From the Author of *Anonymous* & *Sleepin' Wit' the Virus*

THE WRITE MESSAGE

presents

Kreepin' Wit' the Virus

"I have avoided mirrors,
in an effort to avoid the pain associated with my fate…"
—A.L.

Karla Denise Baker

First Edition

The characters and events in this book are fictitious. Any similarity to real persons, living or dead, is coincidental and not intended by the author.

ISBN-13: 978-0615513836
ISBN-10: 0615513832

Printed in the United States of America
10 9 8 7 6 5 4 3 2 1

Avery Love Saga Series by Karla Denise Baker:

Anonymous
Sleepin' Wit' the Virus (a sequel of Anonymous)

E-mail: karlabkr@yahoo.com

Formatting/Editing/ Creative concept: Karla Denise Baker
Photographer: Don Sherrill
Cover model: Karla Denise Baker
Cover graphics: Toni (tirvolino@aol.com)

I wrote this story for those who are open-minded. For those who can see deeper than the words and look inside of my soul and feel compassion—feel something that will make you want to reach out and touch someone who is in dire need of a hug, open ear, or hopeful and helpful words of encouragement.

This book has given me the opportunity to think about a lot of things—my mistakes, my triumphs as well as myself as a woman, mother, friend and writer. The one thing I've understood while writing this book is that freedom, peace of mind, and speaking up for *you* is very important. Honesty plays an important role too. Listening and learning from someone else's mistakes is also significant in this story. This is a story of things we are liable to do, have done, and is possibly thinking about doing. If you can relate to this story, then I feel that the messages that I am trying to convey has made its mark.

Dedication

To *Love*,

You have given me so much of you in so little time.
I just want you to know that I am truly, truly grateful for having
you in my life. You've made a huge impact on me (smiling). Because
of you I now know what love is. Know that I will always love you
and never will I ever forget the joy, respect, patience, and
understanding you have given me.
If I never experience the kind of love we've
shared again, know that I won't be disappointed, at least I've
experienced it once in my lifetime.

Loving you always,

K

Kreepin' Wit' the Virus

Tara Hotel

Parsippany, New Jersey

Four damp feet step out of the shower. A deep, dark-skinned hand reaches for the oversize white Martha Stewart towel and gently pats the beaded water off of my caramel-glazed back. I reach out for the navy-blue towel and pat Christopher Morehouse's broad back. It is about quarter to five. Raindrops are thunderously pounding against the window in the spacious contemporary master bedroom as we lay in a still position in the king-sized bed after indulging in *breakfast*. Normally we have *breakfast* at least four times a week. I mean with our busy schedules it is a priority to please my man. Since my last disastrous relationship I've learned a lot about what men want and also about myself. I've learned that a lonely dick is a straying dick. Let's just say it was an eye-opener after dealing with Eli Jones. That man left a lasting impression on me. And from that I now know how much JaVonna Banks is willing to take and how far I am willing to go when it comes to a man.

Anyway, Christopher and I have only been dating for over a year now. No proposal was ever prompted. And if it were I don't think I would've accepted. The skin on my ring finger had no previous tan line and I wanted to keep it that way. Listen, I had recently reestablished a life for myself and I was not about to commit just on the basis that he knew how to cross the street without a crossing guard. Chris and I seemed content. Why mess-up a good thing with irrelevant traditions? Just because two people live together does not mean that they have to fly off and run to the JP (Justice of the Peace) and get hitched. Well, maybe my mother (God rest her soul) would've seen it that way but not me. Relationships are difficult enough without all the dead weight of rules and regulations and meaningless expectations that neither is willing to follow. So basically *he* and *I* are jus' kickin' it.

We both get out of bed in the nude. I enter the beautiful granite master bathroom first. And then Chris follows. While I am sitting on the toilet peeing, Christopher cuts his eyes over at me with a perplexed look upon his face. I flush the toilet, and step toward the sink and squeeze two dime size drops of liquid soap in the palms of my hands, and massage them into a lather, then rinse. As I am doing this, Chris still has that weird look upon his face. I don't know what came over him. Maybe the scent of another man lingering between my thighs might've had something to do with it. But that was in the past, as far as I'm concerned. He turns the faucet on and leans over the sink and splashes cold water on his face, and then he reaches for his toothbrush and toothpaste and brushes his teeth, while I towel dry my hands. He walks out of the bathroom and walks back into the master bedroom and heads straight for the walk-in closet and reaches for his black trousers and lays them on the edge of the sleigh bed as he cuts his coffee-colored eyes over at me. He speaks assertively like the detective that he is. "JaVonna, exactly how many men have you *fucked*?" He asks with the straightness of face. I merely froze. *Oh, no, he didn't*, I think to myself. Why he is asking me such an inappropriate question, I wonder? I pinch the inner corners of my eyes, flabbergasted. Suddenly, my head and heart is throbbing simultaneously.

"Look, Chris, that's privileged information." I say in the gentlest tone I can muster up looking him dead in his gorgeous face.

"Oh really?" He replies slowly scrolling his eyes up my

7

curvaceous frame as if he is trying to magnify every man's fingerprint that had ever touched me. I cannot believe that we are having this conversation at 5:40 a.m., but we are.

My hands rise in truce. Don't wanna ruin our getaway, yet I cannot disremember his words. There are implications behind his words. Innuendos. I am growing to love this man…doesn't he understand this, I think to myself. I turn to face the full-length mirror that is leaning against the sage-colored wall. I take a good hard look at myself: Coke bottle figure, size two frame, exotic eyes, firm 36Ds, long and shapely legs, and my apple-shaped buttocks. And I think to myself, all of this is exclusively for him. He watches me with disdain in his eyes. Obviously he isn't convinced. And honestly, I do not feel the need to try to convince him anymore. I've done every possible thing to make him feel secure, but suddenly I am feeling uncomfortable in my own skin and it doesn't seem to faze him. I thought coming here would be spontaneous, but it is quite obvious that everything has backfired in my face.

I cannot understand how one minute my pussy was sloppy wet and now dry as my Aunt Irma's carrot cake. We had just made passionate love not even a half an hour ago.

I gape at his muscular nude body and say, "How are you going to ask me how many men have I fucked, huh?" I snap, feeling this urgency to be heard. I run my fingers through my brunette hair, and then cut my nutmeg-colored eyes up to the ceiling and scrunch up my nose because just looking at him disgusts me.

His left hand reaches out for my right hand. I snatch it away. "Don't touch me, Chris! Get…!"

Christopher runs his hands down his face, flustered. "Listen. Sit down for a minute. J, baby, all I asked was a simple need-to-know question." He says while he reaches out for my left hand and pulls it toward him. He then massages my fingers with his long slim fingers that feel like silk against my hot skin. He lifts up my chin trying to portray a sensitive man. "JaVonna, I don't want us to be having dinner at one of our favorite restaurants and some guy comes strolling over talkin' 'bout how he…" I smirk, and then moisten my bottom lip with spittle trying not to shed a tear. Immediately a grimace outlines my face. It is difficult to swallow how he looks at me. We are only dating not on the verge of marriage. Where is this coming from, I wonder? Is it from the fellas on the force? I figured we were good. I mean the phone calls had ceased by our fourth month. The text messages by our sixth. I'll admit it took time for the bitches to get the hint. Christopher also had past lovers still reaching out to him and I voiced my opinion and let it lay. But I guess this is part of the "double-standard" that Michael Baisden was recently talking about with George Willborn. It seems so cliché.

Often I tune in to Baisden's radio show to past the time on my drive home from work. I never really thought that this would be a topic of discussion with any man I dated. I am beginning to see that every man has his pet peeve and I guess this is one of many of Christopher's.

Did Christopher ever consider how those words would affect me especially since our relationship was still in its premature stage? Huh, I can't say. What more do I have to do to convince him that I'm in this for the long haul? I ask myself. What more?

I turn to him and look him dead in his eyes that are filled with coldness as he gapes into mine that are filled with anguish. My chin quivers as I stammer in a melancholy tone, "What…what are you callin' me a *whore*?"

Christopher raises both hands to massage his silky salt-and-pepper hair as well as the contortion away in his chiseled face. He knows just by the look in my eyes and the crackling sound in my voice that he has crossed the line. I have a lot of patience but I have no tolerance for juvenile bullshit. Christopher tries with everything in him to right his wrong but as far as I'm concerned it is minutes too late. The damage has been done!

Christopher gently grabs my upper arms and looks me directly in my red eyes, "No, no, baby. Why would you think that I would ever call you a whore? I never called you a whore. I was just curious that's all," he says, standing his 6'4" bowlegged-self in front of my face and lie. I cannot believe he lied, and so easily too. He places his warm hands on my bare shoulders. Squinting eyes are a clear indication that I am soooo pissed! My body is searing hot and my pussy has moistened to a delicious cream. Too bad he'd just messed-up his second helping of morning fellatio. Dumb ass!

I have to step out of my diva skin just to put a nigga in check. My head sways from side to side, hands meet my 26-inch waist and I let it rippppppppppppppppppp. "You know you got a lot of fuckin' nerve!" Spit spews out of my mouth onto his chin.

Christopher wipes the spit off of his chin with the back of his right hand and tries to reassure me that it is suddenly no big deal. Ohhhhh but is a BIG, BIG, BIG DEAL!!

I didn't give up women for this bullshit. If I woulda known beforehand I woulda taken my chances with this chick named Viktor. But just the thought of her kinda makes me shiver in my skin. Viktor is sexy as hell, so why am I running from her? Honestly, I don't really know. Maybe I'm afraid of what she has to offer…great sex.

I drift back.

"Babe, babe…calm down! It is not that serious. It was just a question." Christopher exclaims, with no regard as to how it makes me feel. It is just a question to him, but it says so much more to me. He has just labeled me. That's where he fucked up.

I cross my slender arms about my chest, tighten my lips trying to compose how I am feeling inside…foolish. Damn! Why'd he have to take me there? Here I am trying to give this man the best of me and he is taking me through all of these changes. I am so close to saying: "Christopher, honey, you got it all twisted. You should be asking me how many pussies have I licked," but I don't want to go there bringing up old baggage. I am trying to be devoted to this man but this is the shit that will turn a chick like me to look the other way and look at all men the same. They are all fucked up. But I don't want to go there because that would be the most inaccurate stereotype. Let's just say that at this moment Christopher is playing himself out and opening the door for someone else to walk right on in, quite possibly another woman.

There is dead silence between us as I am getting dressed in my DKNY sky-blue skirt suit, slip my size eights in my Manalos, grab my Coach bag and matching umbrella, and storm out of the door.

I hop in my red Camry mad as hell as I head home to check on my apartment before heading for my photo shoot in the City.

Once I arrive in Teaneck, New Jersey, I stop at the 7-Eleven to grab a newspaper and a cup of Joe. As soon as I walk into the store I greet the clerk, Jack. "Hi, Beautiful." Jack says with a huge smile on his rotund face. He leans his pudgy body over to grab a cardboard box. "How's my buddy Chris doing?" He asks as he is refilling the Gatorade with his large ivory-colored hands. I really don't want to hear Chris' name right now. I really, really don't. If Jack only knew the shit that went down earlier, huh, he wouldn't be asking me about him neither. I try to make light of things by saying, "Oh, he's fine. Home sleeping," as I reach for a small Styrofoam cup, pour my coffee and grab a lid, walk a few feet and grab a Record newspaper, and walk toward the counter. I pay for my items and head toward the door but before I exit out I yell in a pleasant tone, "See you tomorrow, Jack!"

"Okay, darling, you have you a great day!"

I hop back in my car. As I am making a right onto Teaneck Road a white Range Rover comes backing out of its driveway. I hit the brakes but not quickly enough and my tail end is hit. I pullover and so does the Ranger Rover. I get out ranting and raving in my head as I am walking up to the driver's side window with a salty attitude.

Before I get a word out, the driver's side door opens and a pair of chocolate brown leather shoes steps out in this tall, light-skinned frame of handsome man dressed in a navy-blue business suit.

"Are you okay?" he asks me.

I was hoping that he would've been a complete idiot, but he's not. "Yes, I'm fine." I say.

"Let me see the damage," he says.

We both walk back to my car and he checks the bumper. There's a noticeable dent. The paint is scratched but it is nothing major. I mean nothing to make a big stink about and get the police or our insurance companies involved.

"I'd be happy to get this fixed by my mechanic." The man says, "Unless you prefer your own?"

I'm still frazzled about Chris I really don't care. "No, no, yours is fine." I say.

"I'll make sure you have a rental until it is repaired." He tells me.

He seems to have all the answers, I think to myself. "You seemed in a rush," I say to him.

"I was heading to the hospital. I guess I was distracted."

"Yeah. I know the feeling. The day has just begun and already there is …" I pause, finding myself opening up to him, but he doesn't seem to mind.

"It happens. If you give me your number I can contact you to let you know when you can take your car to my mechanic."

"Sure. It is …" as I am telling him my cell phone number I notice something about him. "Weren't you…?" I wave my right hand. "Oh, never mind."

"You were going to say…"

He looks so familiar, I think to myself.

"Well, I have to get going before I am late for my shoot."

"Are you a model?" he asks, "I mean you're very beautiful. Why wouldn't you be a model?"

"Yes, and I should've been there, like now."

"Well, don't let me hold you up, ah…"

"I'm sorry. My name is JaVonna Banks."

"Nice to meet you. Well under better circumstances, of course." He says with a smile. "Xavier Combs."

Damn. His face just lights up when he says his name.

"Nice to meet you, too." I say to him.

"Well, if you need an alibi, don't hesitate to call me. Oh, let me give you my number." He reaches his hand inside his suit jacket pocket and pulls out a business card. "I'll vouch for your lateness." He says.

He hands me the business card that reads: RED ALERT in big red letters.

"Thanks." I say.

Is he flirting with me? Look at me. Of course he is.

"I'll call you before noon, Ms. Banks."

"Okay." I say, and then head back to my car and get inside.

As I drive off I glance at the newspaper on my passenger seat and there smack dab on the front page is Mr. Combs himself. I nearly run through the traffic light, but abruptly I press my foot on the brake, take a deep breath, and then cut my eyes back over to the newspaper and scroll them down to the article. There it is in dark, black print—a familiar name… Avery Love. Damn. I mumble under my breath. "This bitch is his fiancée!" I squint my eyes. "You gotta be kidding me! Not for long, *bitch*. Not for long."

Xavier

After leaving Holy Name Medical Center I head straight home. I park my white Range Rover in the driveway, exit out with sluggishness, and slowly twist the key to open the front door. As I walk into the house it feels eerie without Avery here with me. It feels empty too even though it is fully furnished. I never really realized how quiet it is around here until now.

I walk into our master bedroom and push "play" with my forefinger on our answering machine. "Xavier, it's JaVonna. Listen, I was wondering if you had any plans this evening. Maybe we can get together for a bite to eat and/or go have a drink at the Z-Bar. Give me a call at my suite. You know the number."

My massive hands run up and down my face, flustered. I'm pushing it by giving her *our* home phone number. I probably would've been better off paying "The Professional Wingman" Thomas Edwards, (the Love Coach) instead of trying to jump back into the dating world on my own. I mean a part of me feels like move on because Avery is not coming back to you. But then the inner part of me says that she is. I'm not trying to mislead JaVonna in any way, but I must admit it feels good to be in the company of a beautiful woman. A woman who is into me for me and who can take my mind away from my problems. She knows how to make me forget, at least for a little while. I like her because she is very subtle about it. Besides, I need a break and JaVonna gives me that with no strings attached. She listens to me babble on and on about work. No. I haven't confessed about my situation…about my love for Avery. She doesn't even know and truthfully I won't share. Why would I do something so insensitive as to bring up another woman with a woman of interest? I'm not one to play on women's emotions. That's not my style. A lot of things never crossed my mind about JaVonna; I'll be the first to admit. I was just so eager to see her and that I did. I saw her in the flesh and she looked delectable.

I stare at the computer screen and playback everything in my head. The window burst into shattered glass—wet blood on my hands—her face—the look of fear in her eyes.

I drift back.

My eyes tear up so I rise to preoccupy my mind. I decide to type in my journal and as I am scrolling through my files I come across an unfamiliar file: Everything That Looks like Her. Maybe I shouldn't invade her privacy, I think to myself. But the inquisitiveness of what she might've wrote piques my curiosity, so I scroll down and begin to read:

2008, 4th November

Dear Sis,

Girl, I haven't had time to buy another journal so here I am typing on this HP computer. Yeah, girl, it's my birthday! Anonymous is my gift to me. I am so excited! I wish Johnnie were here. We'd be painting the town red right about now instead of me sitting here chatting with you and stuffing my gut with this pint of chocolate ice cream. It was a wonderful grand opening. I knew once I got home I would feel blah, though. It's my birthday and I feel lousy. Why? 'Cause I'm alone. No one wants to be intimate with me having this shit running through my veins. No man will even come as close as Zaelyn had. Sis, you see what happened with that after the condom came off. He went on an alcoholic binge. I don't want my man to become an alcoholic after making love to me. I want him to be comfortable in his skin. I know, I know, it wasn't all my doing. Zaelyn had some issues of his own that he needed to address to God and his wife and children. I couldn't believe that he lied just to get some HIV-positive coochie. I guess you can say he got more than he bargained dealing with me, but at least I gave him options. He had a choice. I told him the truth. And yet, he still deceived me. How cruel can one be?

Talk to yah later,

Avery

2008, 5th November

Dear Sis,

I received an unexpected call from my boss Xavier Combs III around 10 p.m., yesterday wishing me a happy belated birthday. It

14

really caught me off guard, you know? I was flattered. Well, at least someone remembered. Someone cared about Avery Love. Wow!

Avery

My hands tremble on the keyboard as I drift in deep thought.
"Yes. Avery…what?"
"Sir, she regained consciousness."
I burst into tears. "Oh, thank you. Thank you for calling. I'm on my way!"

I take a moment to thank the Lord, and then I drift in thought of my past with the troubled DeNetria James.

Me loving DeNetria James was at a time when she was deeply in love with cocaine. Back then I diligently and delicately encouraged rehab but she was too far-gone to pull herself out of the deep hole she had dug. Loving her as I did, I stood by her side until I found myself becoming her supporter. Those eyes of hers used to lure me in and my hands would sink in my pants pockets and pull out my money-clip donating to fulfill her happiness. I began to feel great pain by my actions of being an enabler. I had no alternative but to relinquish myself from her grip. I felt that one-day love would come with another woman, so hopeful that she would be drug-free. And so it seems that has come to pass with Avery.

April 22

I went to the hospital today. There seems to be no change with Avery. She just lays there like she is in a peaceful sleep. Often I feel like shaking her back to me. The impulse rushes through my veins. I don't want to hurt her. Never do I want to purposely hurt her. (Sighing) Um, I met a woman. Ah, her name is JaVonna Banks. This just recently happened. I was fighting within myself, asking myself questions as to why I was even entertaining the thought of seeing her. Something was challenging me to test my love for Avery. Why? Why, am I even questioning my love for her? I mean I've seen plenty of women in passing and some do flirt, some are very upfront about wanting to get to know me, and I've pretty much been the same since Avery and I have been a couple…loyal to my lady. I speak, laugh, but my heart and soul is with her…and only her. So I ponder as to why I even doubt my love for her.

Xavier

I sit for what seems like a minute and then reach for *Anonymous* out of the top drawer of my desk. I skim through the pages:

Pg.18:

I treated Hypnotic like he was the Long Ranger. Yes Sis, that's what I said, Long Ranger because his penis was long as hell! I was attentive and responsive to satisfying his every need. And he reciprocated the same in return. Our lovemaking consisted of rose petals covering the bed, champagne bubble Jacuzzi, warm caramel and much, much foreplay. He caressed me from my feet to the tip of my head. Ooh! I still get goose bumps every time I think about him.

Pg.19:

He would stand before me gleaming, just glossed down with his tan-colored muscular frame all covered in lusciousness. He made my pulse rise and my toes curl. Shoot, they're curling now! Bit-of-Honey was just that, with sweetness. His five-foot-eleven inch of man was adventurous, humorous, and a woman needs a man who can make her laugh. I loved men who were confident, but not arrogant. I didn't mind a man being well-groomed, actually that turned me on. Smelling like he's ready to be licked down.

Pg.20:

LoJac made me feel safe. Gradually I felt my feelings growing for him and then I got scared and faked like my period was late. I guess I felt if he thought that I was possibly pregnant that he would break-up with me. I got panicky; became a sharpshooter with my mouth, and seemed very, very nervous. I gave a hell of a performance. I'll admit STDs; HIV/AIDS were never on my billboard.

Pg.90:

Blu McDowell slithers into my psyche and I replay him slowly taking off his shirt. All I can say to myself is, "Showtime!" I mean, I've seen many men in my day, but Mr. McDowell was an unexpected package with a big red bow tied around him.

Pg.115:

Travar's definitely attractive, with strong features and a whitening smile. His height has to be close to seven feet and his biceps are chiseled. He has long dreadlocks that dangle down his back, but they need a bit of grooming. His goatee is outlined with sharpness on his honey skin. He's a pleasure to look at. And I must say I am lusting as I suck on a piece of apple jolly rancher.

Pg.129:

He unbuckles my shoes and massages my feet. Oh... my... God! The man massages feet. I've died and gone to heaven, for sho'. He starts kissing me on my neck, while his other hand strokes my thigh. My body grows fiery hot. I want to just spread 'em and invite him in. I tease his earlobe and find it's his sensitive spot. Travar moans and I start kissing his neck...

Pg.152:

I am checking Zaelyn out as we walk side-by-side and he looks polished down to his shoes. He is wearing a casual camel linen suit. He has on a soft beige shirt and his dark skin tone brings everything out. Dark chocolate shoes are polished to perfection. His hair is clean cut, and he's nicely shaved, and smells like fresh ocean oil. Woo! Temptation is on my back saying, Chile, whachu gonna do? His dark chocolate is sinfully good 'nough to nibble.

Pg.158:

We leave the club at 3:00 a.m. Zaelyn parks across the street from my apartment building and walk me to the door. He looks deep into my eyes and moves in closer and closer until we bump heads. He sniffs my neck as I maneuver my neck wanting him to do it again. He lays his head right in the crease of my cleavage. I hold him tight not wanting to let go. Pulses rise.

Pg.169:

We lock eyes for a second and then out of nowhere, Danell kisses me on the cheek. A peck on the cheek turns into a peck on my lips. And then a passionate kiss that makes my body flutter. I look Danell in her eyes piercingly; pull her face close to me, swapping saliva. What has come over me?

Pg.178:

Zaelyn lies on top of me and slowly tries to enter my walls, while kissing my neck, breasts, and navel, but the entrance feels cemented. I squint because the pressure is not pleasurable. I feel as if I am a virgin. I inhale with anxiety as he tries to enter for the second time and my eyes close as the walls partially open. I exhale. He is larger than I thought. Then he tries a third time and he strokes once, twice, until the rhythm moves my body along. He palms my shoulders giving him more of grip and spreads my legs with his legs allowing him to have his way. Suddenly, I am in the driver's seat positioning on top riding him forward, backwards, sideways, and in a circular motion. His arms extend on both sides of the bed and he pulls on the comforter for support. Sweat is dripping from my face, down my breasts and onto his stomach. He sits up and I continue to giddy-up horsy on his long, hard, stiff penis. Zaelyn flips me on my stomach and I am taking it doggy style. My head bobs as he thrusts with forcefulness. I moan loudly. That triggers him to go faster, harder, faster, and harder.

Pg.178:

"I'm – c-c-c-, cu-, ccccuuummmmiiinnn'!" I clamp both arms around his neck, tears scream down my face, at that second he releases while our bodies are sticky with our tropical juices. We both lean back wanting a smoke, but settle for a glass of water.

My eyes burn with fury as I smack the book close, toss it back in the drawer, and slam the drawer shut. The phone rings. I flinch in my skin, and then extend out my left arm to reach across my desk to answer it.

"Hello?"

"Xavier? This is Stacy…Stacy Blazman. Your buddy from John

F. Kennedy high school, I looked you up and your number was listed so I decided to give you a call. I hope you don't mind?"

I have to take a moment to think and recapture the name. My left brow rises. "Oh, what's been up man? Gosh, I hadn't heard your name in ages. Where have you been hiding in a cave?" I chuckle.

"Man, something like that. What's been up? Oh, heard you're this big time business man now."

"I wouldn't say all that. I founded a non-profit called Red Alert, ah, back in 1999. You know my sister...um, my sister died."

"Really? Whoa, sorry to hear that. What happened? How did she die?" Stacy asks curiously.

I don't want to share her personal business so I quickly change the subject. "Soooooo, where's the wife and kids?"

"Me? Married, nah man. Kids? Damn, they're everywhere." Stacy chuckles.

"You don't say," I reply.

"Well, what about you big shot?" Stacy says.

"My fiancée is in the hospital."

"I heard about it from my aunt who still lives in Paterson. You remember Nooney, tall, light-skinned chick wit the birthmark of a strawberry on her face. She lived over on E. Holsman Street. They've since demolished her house that sat on the corner. She lives on the east side of town now. Yo, man, that's messed up. Did they catch the person?"

"I don't know."

"That's pretty fucked up."

I lean back in my black leather swivel chair. "Tell me about it. So where're you staying?"

"Maryland. My lady friend lives here."

"Oh. So what have you been doing with yourself, man?"

"A little of this, a little of that, you know how it is. I'm in-between jobs right now wit' this fuckin' recession 'n shit."

"It's tough for everyone, including myself. Keep the faith." I tell him.

"No doubt. I plan on making a visit back home soon. Maybe we can get together?"

"That'll be great. Give me a call when you're in town."

"Will do. You take care of yourself. Pray and let God handle the rest."

"You too."

Stacy

Frederick, Maryland

My head is jerking to the soulful sound of Eric Benét confessing, "Sometimes I Cry," while I am lent back on the tattered burgundy couch with my legs spread wide feeling his pain as well as the wetness from this bitch tongue salivating around the head of my dick. Suddenly Eric's voice dissipates as my mind and body soak in the sound of her blues. Damn. It sounds melancholy like watching a baby drowning. Damn. She's young, black, and fragile as a butterfly.

"Stacy, you like that, baby?" she asks in her baby voice. She is oblivious of what a man has to offer and what she should treasure. She is oblivious of many things especially dealing with a joker like myself. For a moment, I feel pity for her dumb ass but only for a moment. Then I look at her like I look at all the other BITCHES in America and I palm her head like a basketball and force her to deep-throat my shit. She should've known better, but she doesn't. And I surely don't have the time or the patience to try to school her. Nah. It is too late. Jokers like me have already contaminated her. But I'm the worst, because I don't give a fuck about her. When I look down at her sucking my dick all I see is a small feeble person. Po' girl ain't got no dignity left.

***

Paterson-born I was raised in the bitter streets over on the Main. The same ghetto slum that boxer Rubin "Hurricane" Carter was wrongfully convicted of murder and sentenced to do life in prison. The same dude who wrote his memoir, *The Sixteenth Round*. Yeah. We were from this place I called the Gutter. It was like we were from the bottom lookin' up hoping to one day make it out and make something good out of our black asses. Rubin did. Me? Huh, I am still chiseling my way out of the gutter.

One day I heard this familiar voice in my head asking me: Which one are you, son: gentleman, bitch ass nigga or nigga bitch? It sounded just like that same bum that used to sit on the stoop slumped over in front of Gene's Liquors. I was around nine years old when I first met him. His slurred voice had me constantly asking myself, who am I? I don't think I really knew. All I did know was that something happened to me, and it made me think about whom I used to be and who I wanted to be. How I used to treat women. How I looked at women. How I tasted women. How I smelled women. And all of that propelled into a deep seeded hatred for women. I hated women especially weak women. I loathed them with such vengeance.

So long ago I used to be that nice type of dude—a tall, deep (as in poetic), clean-shaven, suit-wearing, debonair nigga. I was the handsomest eligible bachelor in this city of Paterson. Don't get it twisted; I'm still an eligible bachelor. I was the kind a dude a girl wouldn't mind introducing to her mom. The kind of dude her (preacher) dad would be eager to take under his wing to teach me man shit especially after finding out that I didn't have a father figure in my life.

See my grandmother Rose, (on my father's side), raised me. My grandparents on my mom's side died in a fire over on River Street. I was little when that happened. Too little to even remember what they looked like.

I remember my grandmother used to take me to church wit' her every Sunday at Holy Redemption Church. She'd sit there proud, back straight wit' her big fancy lavender church hat on looking like a housemother. She looked clean as a whistle in her lavender dress and white patent leather shoes. Grandma's makeup was flawless. Man, she looked like one of those porcelain dolls. I used to have to wear a suit, tie, and hard bottom black shoes to church. The kind of shoes that made that clicking sound when you walked downs a quiet street like having on Sammy Davis Jr., tap dancing shoes. Everybody had to have known it was me by the clicking sound of my polished black leather shoes.

In church, I couldn't slouch down, chew gum or suck on candy while in church wit' grandma. If I did best believe, I got an ass whooping when we'd get home. She was a stickler for the dos and don'ts in God's house but she was a good woman. Grandma Rose always made sure I had a fresh haircut, though. As far as I can remember that was the only time I wore a suit as a kid unless there was a death in the family. Then I'd have to wear a suit to the wake and funeral.

Grandma Rose was a hefty woman all smothered in creamy white skin. She had hazel eyes of an owl, keen hearing, high cheekbones and she had to have weighed at least three hundred and thirty pounds. She stood about 4'11". But she was tall in stature—a sassy, but lively woman with a great big heart. She used to read me bedtime stories every night even though she struggled with some of the big words. She tried her best to instill good in me. I loved her to death. She was my rock. She was a good Christian woman who took excellent care of me when my black ass mother got caught in the drug scene and abandoned me. My dad, I didn't know much about him other than the fact that I was the spitting image of him. He not being a part of my life told me a whole helluva lot about him. He was a deadbeat. And in my eyes he was dead. I never shed a tear for the sorry ass white mutha— named Pride Benjamin.

Blazman was my mother's maiden name. She never married Pride and I assumed he never asked or maybe he did and she declined because the drugs were more important to her.

I had asked my grandmother a couple of times when I was old enough to understand where my mom was and she'd always tell me she honestly didn't know. Pride wasn't close to his mom, so I never had the opportunity to ask him. He treated her like crap and talked down to her when his father left the family for a slimmer, darker, and more educated woman. They later got a divorce and grandma had been single ever since. She never even dated another man after Pride's father. She seemed content in her life. She never bothered anyone, but was always willing to lend an open ear or a hot meal to someone in need. She was the epitome of strength. The strongest white woman I'd ever come to know and love.

I used to be a comic book geek up until I started hanging in the streets wit' my boys: Bryant Humble, Victor Stash, Thomas Wright, and Lou Bassett. We all attended PS 12. We hung out over on Bunker Hill smoking weed and drinking Johnnie Walker Red. I started doing B & E's by the time I reached ten or eleven. Thomas and I got caught breaking in one of the warehouses and we were sent to juvee in Wayne, New Jersey. Victor, Bryant, and Lou managed to get away. It was the first time I was away from grandma. I think I was there for nearly a year. Being in juvee didn't wake me up, though. Nah. I kept getting into trouble with the law. It drove a wedge between grandma and me. She always had my back, but eventually she cut me loose and let me fall flat on my face. That's when I started to wake-up. When I knew she wasn't there for me. I had disappointed her. I didn't like the way it made me feel or how she looked at me. I didn't like it one bit. So I applied myself in school. I graduated, got accepted in Rutgers in Newark, New Jersey, majoring in Accounting.

I was always good with numbers. I wanted to make her proud and I did when I gained my bachelor's degree. I got a job in New York at a CPA, Lipid and Schwartzman, LLC, on Broadway and W53rd Street. It was my first job. By twenty-three, I got me an apartment. Grandma Rose never wanted me to leave her nest, but I felt it was time for me to stand tall and be the man she knew I could be. As long as I was able to keep a smile on her face, that meant the world to me.

One evening after I had gotten off work I called Grandma Rose and told her that I would be stopping by to visit come Saturday. It was Thursday afternoon when I called her. She sounded so vibrant. Well, come Saturday I'd gone to visit her and she hadn't answered the door. I had my spare key since grandma was up in age. I unlocked the door and called out for her but she hadn't answered back. I checked each room of her one-bedroom apartment and when I got to her bedroom, she was lying in bed sound asleep. That seemed rather peculiar to me because grandma was always an early bird. I took a deep breath and called out her name again and she didn't budge. I didn't want to believe it. I didn't want to believe that my seventy-five year old grandmother had died. But she did. She died in her sleep. She was a good woman so it seemed befitting in my opinion for her to part painlessly. Seeing her in that still state pierced my heart. She was the *only* woman that could breakthrough to my soft spot.

When I arrived back home I felt like someone had beaten a nigga down. I was broken, hurt. Man, anything that equated to pain, I was it. God, I felt so alone during that grieving period. I remember I cried for that woman. She was all I had and she was gone. I went to visit her at Fairlawn Cemetery every chance I got. But then, something changed in me after grandma's passing. I stopped going to visit her gravesite. I stopped, because I had turned into someone I knew she'd disapprove of. Even dead, I couldn't face her. Nah. That was the first time I ever considered myself a coward. Grandma Rose was my earth and my earth was shattering right before my eyes.

See I was that nice type of dude always trying to reason just to keep a woman happy. I never wanted to see a woman cry. I was that soft sucker. I was the kind of dude that opened the door for a woman. I showed her respect. I always walked her to her doorstep. Often cooked her dinner, ran her bubble bath, gave her massages, rubbed her feet, and asked about her day at work. I wrote her love letters "just because" and took her on vacations. She never had to bring her purse with her. Her money was no good to me. I treated her like a black goddess. I made love to her mind and then her body. I mean slow lovemaking—the kind of lovemaking that left a lasting impression of me still being inside of her, after hours of me being away from her. I always aimed to please the woman first. Yeah. I catered to only my black queens. But sometimes I'd dipped in vanilla just to satisfy my taste buds. Yeah. I used to be that dude. That softy that bitches hated! That was back in the day though. Back when I was a gentleman. But all that good etiquette shit quickly turned to bullshit when one bitch played me! Yeah, she woke a nigga up. And I became the bad boy and bitches flocked at my feet like pigeons. Yeah. Bitches created this nigga in me.

Man, she looked like a meatier version of Lisa Nicole Carson. Who? Oh, my bad. Her name was DeNetria James. Remember that actress that played in Devil in a Blue Dress. Maybe you're more familiar wit her role in Jason's Lyric. You know who I'm talkin' 'bout. The chick wit' the big ass titties and long ass braids. You could set her titties on a tray and suck for days. I belly laugh.

Anyway, it was spring of '93, and we were both walking in Neiman Marcus at the Mazza Gallerie mall in Washington, D.C., (I was there on company business) and she caught a brother's eye. I was looking sharp sporting my black fedora with my Murano two-button blazer and flat-front pants enhanced by a pair of bloody red Marc Jacob shoes looking like I had just stepped out of a Versace magazine. This fine honey walked like she was worth millions. A confident woman is most definitely a turn on for any man, unless he's gay. Then she becomes competition. Damn was she some fine chocolate for me to admire. It was no coincidence. Nah. I never believed in coincidences. It was fate.

I walked over to her smooth like Denzel and introduced myself in a Hill Harper tone. "Hi. My name is Stacy Blazman." She smiled showing all of her thirty-twos, "DeNetria James," she said all soft and sensual like. I found out if she was married or had a man. "No, I'm single, but I do have two small children," she replied. I laughed inside because I knew I had just struck gold. I remember telling her, "Not for long." I was a confident brother. I had a good head on my shoulders. I knew how to treat a woman like a woman. My grandmother, bless her soul, raised me right. Not only did I know how to make my woman look sexy I knew how to make her feel sexy too. I just kept gassing her head up until she believed that Sam Cooke shit. I had that chick eating out of the palm of my hands. And within two weeks time I had that chick smellin' her own ass.

As I got to know DeNetria I started seeing some things that I didn't notice in the beginning. For one, I ain't have her smellin' nothin'. Nah. She was already a conceited bitch. DeNetria had mad confidence for a big chick. I just didn't know it. That chick took a brother through some serious changes though. Unnecessary shit. She loved drama. And every time she'd get off she wanted to fuck after. She was like fire and she burned a brother real, real bad because I loved her. I mean I truly, truly loved her. I never told any other chick that in my entire life. It took me about a year and half to get her out of my system. A nigga failed because she was still in my system. Talk 'bout doing a nigga dirty. Huh, I wasn't a nigga back then, but DeNetria was the first *bitch* to create one in me.

Once I started treating DeNetria like the slut that she was she loved a nigga up. Shit blew my mind. She schooled a brother real quick. And I transformed seemingly overnight. You got that shit right, huh, all that romantic shit I threw out of the fuckin' window. Within a few weeks I broke that bitch down to my level. Had her kissing my feet, pecking my pinky toe, rubbing my back, and sucking my cock. I felt like a king. Then I kicked that stupid bitch to the curb.

I didn't give a fuck about DeNetria's wants as long as I got what I wanted. Back then; what I wanted was to break that bitch. I didn't wanna hear her mouth unless she was sucking my third arm. That's the only sound I wanted to hear, a slobbering tongue slipping and sliding up and down my nigga. Other than that she could keep her comments to herself. I didn't have time to listen to no gibber-gabber. Listen to her talkin' 'bout her baby daddy. Her who? Baby daddy! Nah. Keep that family shit to yourself. My time is valuable. Either we gonna fuck or you can get the hell out of your crib so that I can call another bitch over to suck my *nigga*.

As it may sound, I don't give a fuck about these *hoes* out here. You see I'm not the type of brother who is trying to woo bitches out of their panties. I say why waste your time putting 'em on. Just come out assed out. Show the freak in you. Don't keep her hidden behind closed doors. A brotha' of my caliber wanna see what you made of. No, my patience is not manufactured for all this lovey-dovey shit. Nah. Wrong nigga. I just come wit' it. Truth be told, these bitches out here love a brotha' up. They say I keep it real. I do. They say I got it going on. I do. They say you da man. I am. I'm everything but a fuckin' joke, bitches. I'm that smooth and sweet shit talkin' brotha' you bitches like, but I can care less about what you want, how you feel, your worries, woes or insecurities. Save that shit for Oprah, Wendy Williams and Mo'nique. Keep it to your damn self 'cause I don't wanna hear it. I don't wanna know. I'm keepin' it real when I say that shit. Fuck you! Pussy comes in all different flavors and in all different shades. It's easy to find another gullible bitch that will bow down on her knees and suck my shit. (Nodding my head up and down...) Trust a nigga on that.

Yeah, I've lost total respect, confidence, and loyalty in worthless bitches. Ya'll come out here all dolled up and ain't got shit! Fake ass bitches! Talk that bullshit like you all educated and dumb as hell. Got several baby daddies and some of ya'll done screwed so many niggas you don't even know who the hell the *real* father is. Ah, ah, ah, bitches, you don't know so stop guessing. Got niggas paying child support for a seed that ain't even his. What kinda mess is that? Trying to trap a brother, huh? And ya'll have the audacity to badmouth a nigga like myself. I'm hurt. (Laughing) No. I'm not 'cause I'm the infamous nigga bitch and don't ya'll forget it. Nigga bitches don't get hurt they do the hurtin'.

Answer this for a slowpoke nigga like me; where'da hell is the real bitches at, huh? What... you so busted that a nigga can't see the real you? Wassup wit' that? How da hell am I 'sposed to know who da hell I'm humpin' if you don't show me the real you? I'm sayin' one minute you Kasha, then you Michelle, what da f—! Where y'all at, huh?

My other gripe is these rainbow-wannabe-lesbian-bitches. Look, either you like dick or you like pussy, which one is it? Don't come chillin' wit' me. Fuck me. And then, two days later after we done fucked you slobbering on some chick's pussy like its aiight. That shit ain't a'ight. Tell a muthafucker that you like pussy too so that we can do the damn thang. I ain't got no problem sharing, you feel me? Keep it real wit' me. I ain't your average nigga. 'Cause I ain't shit. And even though you hum-dumb-bitches know that I ain't shit it don't stop you from fuckin' wit' me. Why? 'Cause your bitch ass is addicted to my dick! Can't get enough of my (gripping my joint) Nigga. Lol.

Look, its simple mathematics for you slowwww bitches. When I come over to your crib I expect your kitchen to be clean. I expect it to be sooooooo clean that I can lick the floor without getting pubic hairs stuck in-between my teeth. Don't you bitches know how to shave? Ain't nothin' worse than having a chick whose pussy got an afro-puff. Nappy-headed bitches!

When I come over I expect my food on the table piping hot. I want it to be mouth watering. And it better taste good too because I might want seconds and thirds, but if your ass can't keep the friggin' kitchen clean, I'm out! And on my way to the next bitch crib in your ride! (Grinning…).

(Sippin' on Remy). You just reminded me of something. DeNetria used to sweat a nigga. I had her wide the fuck open especially when I ate her out. She was a hefty hoochie momma, but she had a cute face, humongous titties and a doublewide ass. Shit. The bitch was big. But DeNetria could clean a motherfucking kitchen. That chick knew how to make me feel like a fuckin' king. For DeNetria to be a big chick she knew how to keep her swollen pussy smellin' like fresh daisies. I gotta give it to her. She used to use the FDS spray. Douche. That feminine powder shit. Whatever it took to keep the pussy fresh, she would go above and beyond the call of duty for her nigga. But the one thing I hated about that fat bitch was that DeNetria could not fuck worth a damn. Every time I would get in between those ham hock thighs of hers I would get thigh burn. I ain't lying. Every time I would stick my dick in her pussy I'd get dick burn because her pussy was dry as hell. She was drying the fuck up and I couldn't understand why. I figured I'd go and get some KY gel but I said fuck that I'd use it on someone else. Instead I spat on my dick to lubricate it and then I fucked her. And I told, I mean I warned her that if she got pregnant I'd beat the baby outta her. I wasn't fuckin' playin' either. And she knew it too. I fucked that bitch so much the bitch lost weight. I ain't lyin'. And once she did that it was a wrap. I couldn't be wit' her skinny ass anymore. I like the big and beautiful bitch. Not some scrawny toothpick looking crackhead.

DeNetria wouldn't take no for an answer so I had to get ill on her. I hate to say it but I had to slap a bitch backup a size. She needed to be found because she was disappearing right before my eyes. Where you at? I would ask her. Where the fuck you at? I can't see you. You hungry…eat something bitch. Eat something so that I can fuck that fat ass again. Lol.

I am a late-fifty-year-old nigga. I do what da fuck I want to do. I know I can't seem to get a grip on my dick. Nigga loves himself some pussy. It ain't all about the pussy, though. Look, I had a business—a recording studio. I gave that shit up when I got this twenty-two year old chick from Richmond, Virginia, named Charity Fokker pregnant. I dropped everything all because that white bitch was going to file child support on me. Of course my whole persona changed. I know now that it was a dumb move, but I wasn't thinking rationally at the time. All I knew was that I had to bounce. So I did. It ain't no secret that I am addicted to the streets, women, and money. I've always been this way—must be in my genes or something. I loved livin' the fast life, makin' that fast cash, and manipulating bitches for personal gain. It was a job to me—a job that took much innovation and concentration to punk these bitches to get their dough. I had to entertain, put forth effort and energy and charm as well as stamina because these were some needy bitches I was dealing wit'. 'Ey I didn't get the title: *White Knight* for nothing. You had to have gift of gab and lots of it because some of these bitches were educated women. Some had been through hard times and faced bad relationship so they weren't as easy to play as the ones who were uneducated and gullible. It took work. I mean hard work, and I was the most qualified nigga for the job.

Asbury Richardson who happened to be DeNetria's so-called girl, yeah aiight, knew it to be true because, she too, had been in a similar situation with me. But that was 'sposed to be our dirty little secret. Yeah, Asbury, the short, round, deep-dark chocolate chick wit' the wide hips and ass to match and those juicy lips and come-'n-get-dis-pussy-nigga-eyes could get downright dookey-stank-dirty for a nigga. Asbury knew what da fuck was up if she wanted anymore of my dick. That's right. Shut da fuck up and open those legs for a nigga, bitch. And make sure you got my motherfuckin' money, too.

Listen, my philosophy was that sometimes you had to be sly as a muthafuckin' fox and do things that were beneath you to accomplish your goals in life. Because a nigga bitch would either dupe you or soup your head up, hate you or love you. Leave you or fuck you, whichever; a nigga bitch would almost always come out on top.

***

DeNetria is tired of being broken, disappointed, and dismissed by me. Yeah, I know it, but I don't seem to care. What more does a chick like DeNetria has to do to get through to a nigga like me? I mean she's working a 7-3 shift as a nurse's aide. Sometimes she even pulls doubles just to make ends meet. She goes to church every Sunday, with the exception of the days she has to work. She pays her tithes even though she can't really afford to. She is a good mother making sure her kids come before anything she wants or needs. She keeps the house tidy. She cooks every day. And makes sure I get my diva chocolate on the regular. She lets me bust that cherry even when she doesn't feel like it just to keep me happy. Or, maybe she does it just to keep me so that her kids would have a fuckin' father. And when her period comes on she makes sure I'm pleasured, if you know what I mean. Who can ask for anything more? I guess I can. My eyes always tell a lie. I don't have an honest bone in my body. Don't nobody care that I have good looks. Looks fade, and then what? Exactly. I am never satisfied. I am always sharp wit' my tongue. I purposely make DeNetria feel small and unappreciated. Shit! DeNetria don't need me! The girl is gorgeous. Her 5'5" frame and almond brown eyes is a magnet for a muthafucka. She has long, thick hair that is hers. And her body, aw man, she has curves in all directions. No, she's not a skinny chick, but she can pull any man in her bed, but that ain't her style. She has too much respect for her kids and herself to be dragging another make-believe baby daddy into her home, just to say she has a nigga. Nah. That's not DeNetria. She has too much going for her. But see I know how to break a bitch down. Yeah, it's pretty fucked up, but again, I don't care. See the way I tell it I'm pulling rank in her castle. Pulling that paper in and handling those bills and paying child support even though I live here—trying to make myself look like, "The All-American Nigga Bitch." That's what I have my boys thinking. Rrrriiiigghhhttt. You know how nigga bitches do. Always trying to shine and make the chick look like a dumb ass. Truth be told, if it weren't for DeNetria I wouldn't have a bed to fuck my other bitches in. True dhat!

On the real, DeNetria isn't sure what to do when it comes to me, because for one I just recently resurrected from the dead. I played ghost for years, and then, one day I popped up on her doorstep begging to come back. I was always a deadbeat, but DeNetria figured for her two kids that "we" have she'd give me another chance hoping things would work for the better. That was wishful thinking on her part, because I knew that I was the same dog I'd always been.

Truth be told, I was on the run ducking from this other bitch husband that I had fucked a while back. Her husband was a retired cop on the haunt to kill my ass. You could only play for so long until your ass got popped. I knew my days were being numbered.

(Sip, sip, sip, sipppp.) Damn this Remy must be gettin' to a nigga. Oh, let me drop this bomb while I'm feelin' nice. The two kids that we have that I claimed weren't mine. No joke. I said and I quote. Wait! Wait! (Snickering... Lemme make sure I get it right): "Them black ass, ugly ass muthafuckers ain't mine. I'm sterile. I'm shooting blanks. Them black ass, ugly ass muthafuckers ain't mine!" But DeNetria found out that I had more "black ass, ugly ass muthafuckers" out here that I claimed ain't mine. Why did DeNetria take me back? (Chuckling) Must you ask? Aiight. If you insist…the bitch took a nigga back because she wanted to have a family like any other mother. DeNetria felt her kids deserved to have their father if I wanted to be their father. She wouldn't deprive them of my love. She wouldn't hold grudges. She wouldn't punish the kids because of how she felt about me. She loved her kids dearly and would give her life for them. They were her kids and she'd never abandon them. She didn't care how hard her struggles might have been she'd starve for them. And if she had to pimp her pussy just to put food on the table, she would without giving it a second thought. DeNetria is a devoted mother. And I can vouch for that. She is a goodhearted person. We have a lot in common. I mean her upbringing was of a single parent household. Just like me. Her father jetted before she could even talk. Just like me. She figured the man of her dreams wouldn't be like her invisible dad. How wrong was she, because that's exactly the kind of man she attracted…a nigga bitch, which happens to be me.

Yeah. I say that because any man who is calling himself coming back just so that he won't have to pay child support is a nigga bitch in my eyes. Oh, I tried that gift of gab on her. Tried bringing gifts home like expensive Chanel perfume. Shit, I knew she liked. I tried wooing her in bed, in the shower, in the kitchen, in the living room, to keep her floating on a cloud. I licked her pussy and ass during those desperate times when I thought I almost had her to go down and stop the child support payments. But to my surprise, she didn't. She saw right through my little charade. And once I couldn't get my way, the blows pounced on her ass. I beat that bitch down like a madman right in front of her fuckin' kids, and dared her to call the police. What kind of shit was that! But then come a few days later, I'd want to act like she was my trophy in front of my boys. And what did she do? Oh, that bitch played along like I told her to. She knew what was best for her. Or she'd catch a bullet right between those pretty eyes of hers.

Xavier

"Red Alert, Xavier Combs, speaking. Hello, Dr. Hooverman. How's my lady doing today?"

"About the same. Nothing's changed," Dr. Hooverman says, in a sort of tiring tone. "I pulled a double shift just thought I'd give you a call before I head home for some sleep."

I lower my head, squeeze my eyes tightly, and sigh. "Okay, okay. Well keep me posted. Thanks for returning my call." My quivering hand places the phone back in its cradle. I stand and walk towards the window and gaze out, seeing the world, hearing the commotion of the busy streets, and feeling numb inside. I try to compose my emotions. Try to convince myself that this is not happening to me. My hands massage my scalp in a back and forth motion. My lady, my woman, my future wife is lying in the hospital in a coma because some sick person didn't want her to be happy, so now we have to suffer. It's not fair, but what can I do? What can she do? It's out of both of our hands. I lower my head, and as I do I hear a familiar voice say, "Pray, brother, pray." My eyes get misty. I swear it sounds like my baby sister.

Am I losing my mind, I ask myself as I make my way back to my desk and sit down, lean back in my chair, thinking about sexy JaVonna. I hit the speaker button on my phone. "Marilyn, I'll be stepping out of the office for the rest of the day. Should anyone call just take a message, okay."

"Will do, Mr. Combs."

Crenshaw

DAY 1: "Ms. Love, my name is Detective Crenshaw. Can you hear me?"

Silence.

DAY 2: "Ms. Love, my name is Detective Crenshaw. Do you know who shot you?"

Silence.

DAY 3: "Ms. Love, my name is Detective Crenshaw. Did you have any enemies? Anyone you can think of?"

Silence.

DAY 4: "Ms. Love, my name is Detective Crenshaw. Did you see anything usual the day before? Ms. Love, can you hear me?"

Silence.

3 weeks later...

DAY 21: "Ms. Love, my name is Detective Crenshaw. Can you hear me?"

 Silence.

DAY 22: "Ms. Love, my name is Detective Crenshaw. Do you know who shot you?"

Silence.

DAY 23: "Ms. Love, my name is Detective Crenshaw. Do you know who shot you? Did you have any enemies? Did anyone threaten you in the past?"

Silence.

3 years later…

DAY 1088: "Ms. Love, my name is Detective Crenshaw. Do you know who shot you? Did you have any enemies? Did anyone threaten you in the past?"

I come to.

Silence.

DAY 1089: "Ms. Love, my name is Detective Crenshaw. Can you hear me?"

AVERY: "Yes." I say in a slow, raspy tone.

CRENSHAW: "Do you know where you are?"

AVERY: My eyeballs roll in my head. "Yes, a hospital?"

CRENSHAW: "Do you know where Xavier Combs III is?"

Silence.

CRENSHAW: "Ms. Love, do you know where Xavier Combs III is. Isn't he your fiancé?"

AVERY: (swallowing hard, eyes welling up). My eyes surveillance the room as this sharp pain pierces my heart. My voice is low and feeble. "He's not here." I say hearing my voice crack. God, it hurts to have to admit this to a total stranger, but I'm not one to lie. Crenshaw gapes at me with perplexity in his face. "When was the last time you saw Mr. Combs, Ms. Love?" he asks me. I pause, and then answer as I see a flashback in my head. I remembered hearing myself scream. I remembered the burning sensation throughout my body. I remembered so vividly the blood. "The day of the shooting," I say.
CRENSHAW: "Do you remember the year that the shooting occurred?"
AVERY: I close my eyes, and then release a hollow breath. "No."

Avery

Six months later

It is about noon on an autumn Sunday. "Hear My Call" by Jill Scott dominates the anguish that is swarming throughout this small apartment and inside of me. My turquoise nightgown is clinging to my skin like the ache in my heart. And as I look down at my bare feet they remind me of my journey and destinations—the places I've been and the places I wish to be. I lean on the left side of my body, putting pressure on myself to stand with the help of this steel walker to support me while I am still recuperating from my gun shot wounds. I can only stand for a few minutes at a time. I tell you I feel like an older woman—much older than forty-five. My body has gone through a lot, but the in-patient and outpatient physical therapy has really helped me regain my strength back. Physically, I still have a long ways to go. Emotionally, I feel like I am on the verge of a nervous breakdown. Spiritually, I am beneath contempt for myself. "Yes, Avona, your girl has most definitely lost her way this time," I say aloud. I swear I can hear Avona say, Avery, your life is a revolving door of heartache and despair. I'd drink to that, I think to myself as my eyes glance over at the book lying on the kitchen table that I have every intention of reading, *Black Love Signs* by Thelma Balfour, to see whom I'm most compatible with because it is quite obvious that I have some deep seeded issues when it comes to men.

The day that I was discharged from Holy Name Medical Center was the scariest days of my entire life. I wanted to die, but God reassured me that I would get through the pain just like everything else in my life. I could not believe that Xavier left me in my worst state of being. I could not believe that he deserted me. The same man who professed his unconditional love for me—the same wonderful man who asked for my hand in marriage. The man who practically worshipped the ground I walked on even knowing that I am HIV-positive. I tell you I could not fathom what transpired between the two of us. I don't want to deal with the reality of not having him in my life. I don't want to deal. I sigh, wondering what could've happened.

To distract my thoughts I resume back to what I was doing. It has been a long time since I made a home cooked meal. How long? I don't quite remember. The aroma of seasoned turkey wings, macaroni and cheese, and fresh cut string beans flow in the small kitchenette as well as my thoughts.

"Hello."

"Helloooooooo," Xavier sounds so chipper. "Where are you?"

"Oh, at the house cooking dinner, I've been up since 8:00 a.m., just finished coming back from the Laundromat. I stopped and picked up some groceries, came home and felt like whipping up a meal for us."

"Uh-huh. I'm just leaving the golf course."

"How are you doing?" I ask.

"I'm fine. Just thought I'd give you a call before I head home. I'll make me a sandwich once I get there because I didn't eat breakfast this morning."

"Me neither. It's nice out today. After I finish cooking I'll probably go for a walk."

"Okay. Well, I call you later to see if you need anything while I'm out playing the pick-it."

"Okay." I say with a huge smile on my face.

"Okay, chef, go back to what you were doing. I'll talk to you later. I love you."

"I love you, too."

That was the last conversation I remember having with Xavier. I don't know exactly how long ago that was, but that's all I remember. If it weren't for his name and cell phone number in my address book I wouldn't even have it. I think the man has vanished off the face of this earth. All of a sudden I feel nauseous anticipating Xavier's call. It is about 7:51 p.m., when I finally call him. I get his voicemail so I leave a message: "It's close to 8:00 p.m. I assume that you aren't coming." I wait and wait for him to call back, but he never does. Around 10:00 p.m., I call Xavier back, and again I get his voicemail: "Um, is there something you haven't told me…something I need to know? Maybe it's me, but my gut tells me that something…" I wait and wait again, still no callback. Around 12:20 a.m., I call him again. This time I am beyond worried. My eyes begin to well up. The thought of losing him really frightens me. I feel alone and disregarded as if I mean nothing. Not even good enough for a callback. I mean our love meant something to me, but for a second or maybe a minute I question his love for me. He knows that I am a worrywart, so why have me worrying, huh? It doesn't make any sense to me. Beep!

"I just need to know that you are okay. I hope nothing has happened to you. Please call me and let me know something. This is not like you not to call me back. Don't leave me hanging like this. Please call. I feel I at least deserve an explanation. Yes, it's me, Avery."

After my meltdown, I still receive no callback from Xavier. My eyes meet the ceiling and I think to myself, this vacant place is most familiar to me. Yes, I've been here before. God, it reminds me of Johnnie. I blink, and then try to block the thoughts out of my head, so quickly they dissolve. Calm myself; he'll call, I think, but deep down I feel just the opposite. He's never going to call…according to my calendar; it's been…. Why do I keep holding on?

***

I get up, get dressed in some lounge wear, pull out my electric-blue shopping cart and load a bag of clothes to go to the Laundromat across the street from where I currently live. As I am entering the Laundromat I see a woman who resembles someone I know, but she's dressed in some baggy clothes that she's swimming in. Every five seconds she keeps checking herself out in her compact mirror: eyes, nose, neck, cheeks, and hair. Every time someone enters the Laundromat, she's checking herself out in the reflective door. No. It can't be, I say to myself. But to my surprise, it is Teka Miller. You know who Teka is…the size zero chick I told you about. TEKA! C'mon. Teeeeekkkkkkaaa the skinny chick with the big ass rock on her finger, remember. I told you about her. Remember I saw her while I was getting my mail. She had on her workout gear looking like she smelled funky. Teka…the same chick, who for the life of me, could not stop bragging about being engaged to her mystery man, ah, ah, what's his name? Yessss, her!

As soon as Teka sees my baldhead and me she waves. I am like, oh shit; it's her, damn. Of course I play the long-time-no-see-girl role. Look I hadn't seen her in a while so I didn't want to be nasty. I notice Teka looks different, other than the obvious of her being a bony twig. I mean she looks the same but not quite the same, if that makes any sense. And the big ass ring is not on her ring finger. What! Yeah, she is not wearing her 5-carat oval diamond ring. Somebody

36

must've gotten dumped. I smirk. What happened? I dunno, but I am sure as hell gonna find out.

"Hello Teka."

"Hi Avery, how've you been?"

"Oh, I'm blessed," I reply, but do I really feel blessed, I have to ask myself.

"Hmmm, blessed, huh," Teka repeats, rhetorically.

I just look at her because she has this strange look in her eyes. Something I haven't seen with her before. What gives?

"Are you okay, Teka?" I ask her.

"You know something, Avery…this is the first time we've ever had a conversation that didn't last more than two syllables."

I know she's right because as you know I can't stand her. I shrug my shoulders because it is the god's-honest-truth. Back then, I had no interest in getting to know Teka because she annoyed me something terrible. I was so used to being alone, not wanting anyone to crowd my space. Having a girlfriend…I tried that with Danell and that turned into something I never saw coming. Often I think about Danell, but I don't have the nerve to contact her. Why stirrup old baggage.

There is a moment of silence between Teka and me. I walk over to the washer and load my soiled clothes. Walk over to the change machine and slip in a five-dollar bill. Gather my change and walk back to my washer to start the wash as I am filling the bins with Tide with Bleach and Downy. The TV is blasting in Spanish and I notice this Puerto Rican man staring at me. Hasn't he ever seen a baldhead woman before, I wonder? I suck my teeth. Boy, I can't stand men gawking at me like I'm some alien from outer space. As the machine is filling with water I walk back over to Teka to chat, might as well use my time wisely.

"Mm-hmmmm." Teka hums.

"Did you say something," I ask her.

"No, just humming." Teka cuts her eyes over at me. It kind of makes me feel uncomfortable. "You ever think about dying?" she says nonchalantly.

Where'd that come from, I wonder?

I am at a loss with Teka's question that sprung out of nowhere. It seems so odd and eerie.

"Ah, not re-cently," I haltingly say. "Are you planning on going somewhere?" I ask her. Not that I really care if she does. I know that was harsh, but you know how I am. Oh no! Who does that sound like? Oh darn…Brick.

"Sooner than I think," Teka says, "it's a shame that we've never become friends, you know. It's good to have a least one good friend you can call your best friend, you know. You ever had a best friend, Avery?" Teka looks at me with somberness in her teary-looking eyes.

I smirk, because now I really feel uncomfortable. Teka continues to speak before I can get a word in edgewise.

"A friend in need is a friend indeed," Teka says, with a melancholy expression on her narrow face.

"To answer your question Teka, yes, I had a best friend named Johnnie."

"Well, I guess you really are blessed, huh?"

"Why do you say that?" I ask her.

"Because all of my forty years I have never had anyone I could consider to be a best friend. I've had acquaintances, associates, but never a best friend. Sometimes I wonder if there is something wrong with me."

At this odd moment I can completely relate to how Teka feels. Since being raped, and especially after Dr. Fulmore told me that I have HIV, and especially after being shot, my perceptions of myself have changed. At one point in my life, I didn't know who I was or what my purpose on this earth was either. I was oblivious of a lot of things. And the only person who seemed to bring me out of the dark shadow of myself was Xavier. Why I can't seem to forget him and move on? Well, because I don't want to forget him. Xavier is a good man. He has a soul that isn't afraid to show its emotions. And I truly love that about him.

Immediately my eyes tear up and my chin begins to quiver. Just thinking about him does something to my insides.

"Are you okay, Avery?" I hear Teka say.

I try to compose myself as I nod my head, yes, but deep down God, I miss my man.

JaVonna

I'm beyond the dyke phase. That's right, I said it! Yeah, I've since upgraded since Danell. Although the new me haven't changed much. I still like it creamy, sticky, and kinky. You gotta come right fuckin' with a chick like me 'cause I like my pussy to hurt. I like it to throb. I like it to purrrrrrr and talk when it comes to being stroked.

See I do more than the average ghetto-chick. I observe a lot and listen to what these trifling bitches have to say about what they supposedly don't do like giving head and eating pussy. These bitches out here lie up a friggin' storm. I don't believe anything they say. It's just a bunch of bullshit because at the end of the day you're going to do what is necessary to keep your man or woman happy. They know damn well that behind closed doors they be sucking 'em dick and licking the hell outta those pussies. Personally I think every woman should indulge in giving head and licking pussy. I'm just that way when it comes to pleasing my wo-man. I'm also the type of chick that likes competition especially from a nigga that talks about what he's going to do to me. The ones who hype their shit up like they're God's gift to women, they're my favorites. You know how it goes: "Baby, you can't handle all of this here dick", "Girl, I'll make your pussy talk", "I'll fuck you so good you'll sign over your pussy-rights to me," blah, blah, blah. I get a kick out of the niggas who got all that mouth and can't back it up. I let 'em know straight up that they fucked up messin' wit' a chick like me. Then I'd step and give 'em something to think about. Shit, ain't no shame in JaVonna Banks game. I don't have time for no slow-pumpin'-non-fuckin' nigga who can't handle his business. And I especially don't have time for the niggas who start whining like little bitches after I done turned their muthafuckin' asses out. I keep tellin' these fools that all bitches ain't the same. Some of us got skills. Having a pussy is one thing, but having a pussy that does tricks is another. Every woman wishes that she could do what I do. But unfortunately we aren't all blessed this way.

I mastered fucking to an art form. Once I put my inscription on these niggas they forget how to act. That hardcore role becomes obsolete. Listen, I already know that I'm a piece-of-work, but I don't boast about it to the world. Some things are better left unsaid, you know. See I don't need anyone to validate me. I know what the fuck I got between these legs of mine…first class pussy. The kinda pussy that will make a nigga weak. Look it does not take Stevie Wonder to see that I got these slow-pumpin' niggas where I want 'em. These knuckleheads used to be sending me flowers, giving me money, leaving love notes on my doorstep, buying me jewelry, paying my cell phone bill, car note, rent, and buying me shoes, clothes, getting my hair and feet done and leaving stupid ass messages on my voicemail like they in love or something. I really didn't do anything but take my frustrations out on 'em. All they heard was psssssssssssssssssssssss comin' out of my sweet pain pussy. And niggas went berserk. 'Ey they got the game all twisted to mean more than what it was. It was merely a fuck to me. Good fuck, but fuck, nevertheless.

Whether you care to know it or not I have slowed down tremendously. I was ready to be in a monogamous relationship after my breakup with Danell. A few months later I met the down-to-earth Eli Jones. He was light-skinned with velvety black mane and smoldering good looks. Eli was a Navy man stationed in Norfolk, Virginia. Eli lured me in with those Luther Vandross lyrics and Smokey Robinson pussy melting eyes. OMG! His hazel eyes used to have me slobbering JaVonna juice in my panties. I'd fallen head-over-heels for that man. Too bad he didn't feel the same for me. I mean Eli used to make me cum so hard I'd damned near lost my tastes for women.

After a while of dealing with Eli, something changed in me. He became a special part of my life. Yes, I became one of those women. I tried to please him. I did things for and with him that I didn't do for or with any other man. Okay, I'll admit, I was gullible. Whatever it took to keep him happy I was willing to give all of me. And I did. I was too busy stroking his ego as well as his eight inches (well, actually, five inches when it was shriveled up), while he continued to feed my mind more bullshit. Eli showed me what he was really made of—all 6'6" of him.

Nearly two months into our relationship I received an anonymous call from some chick that claimed that I was fucking her man. I confronted Eli and of course he denied it. When Eli made his three-month visit to Paterson, New Jersey, he had no words for me. He grabbed his navy-blue duffel bag, shoved what clothes he had at my house in it, and walked out of my life. I ran to the window and watched him get into this white Mercedes with this cougar bitch in the driver's seat sticking her middle finger up at me. I felt a pain so sharp in my chest I thought I was going to have a conniption. I stormed into the bathroom, locked the door, sat on the toilet seat, and cried like my mama had just died all over again.

I'll admit, I assumed I was his one and only. I should've known better. But I was desperately looking for love in all the wrong places…the Internet. Yep. I met Eli on Tagged. For nearly four months I stayed on a regimen of me. By the six month I was back on Tagged. That's when Christopher requested me as a friend.

My cell phone rings.

"Hello?"

"JaVonna, its Xavier."

"Hey, baby."

"I-I was wondering if you had any plans this evening?"

"What did you have in mind?" I ask with a sly grin on my face.

"Well, a friend of mine invited me to see the debut of her play. I called to see if you might want to accompany me."

"A play?" I purse my lips, thinking b-o-r-i-n-g.

"My friend is a writer and director. She wrote this script and decided to showcase the premier at Bergen PAC (Performing Arts Center) on North Van Brunt Street in Englewood, New Jersey. She called to ask if I would come out to show some support. So would you like to go?"

I suck in my cheeks with my tongue. I roll my eyes because I do not want to be bored out of my fuckin' mind with this dude and his wannabe another *Raisin in the Sun* or *The Color Purple* bullshit. I exhale. I clench my teeth and say, "Yes."

"Great! I can come pick you up at 7:00 p.m." Xavier says.

I spread my eyes wide, girl, think. Hurry up, J, I say to myself. You can't let him know exactly where you live.

"Ah, Xavier, how 'bout I meet you there. Just give me the address."

"Sure. It's …"

"Okay. See you at 7:00 p.m."

We hang up and I wipe the sweat beads off of my forehead with the back of my right hand. As soon as I do, in walks Christopher through the front door looking like a deep dark chocolate Hershey bar. Looking all good and shit in his Men's Warehouse business suit. My pussy starts to throb so I pull down my thong and invite him in for some J-Juice.

Avery

7:02 A.M.

I wake-up with tears saturating my eyes and nervousness swarms throughout my body. I gape at the clock, and then reach for my cell phone to retrieve old messages Xavier left on my voicemail. Apparently I must've saved them from before. Hearing his voice soothes my pain. God, I need to hear from him. I yearn to see him standing before me, but I know that that is near impossible because he seemed to have dissipated from my life.

My fingers press the 10-digits on my cell phone and on the other end a woman with a soft-spoken voice picks up, "Holy Name Medical Center."

"Can you tell me if you admitted a Xavier Combs III?" I ask her.

"What's the last name, again?" she asks.

"Combs III." I say, releasing a hollow sigh.

"Hold please?"

"Okay."

"Hello, ma'am, there's no one admitted by that name. Let me transfer you to emergency."

"Okay."

"Emergency!" This fast-talking woman answers excitedly.

"Hello. Can you tell me if you admitted a Xavier Combs III?"

"Combs, you said, right?"

"Yes ma'am."

"No ma'am."

"Okay, thanks."

I end the call with emptiness embedded in my heart. All I can think is that Xavier is deserted somewhere. And all I want to do is search high and low for his love. Scream out his name and hope that he screams back. All I want to do is bring him back to me. All I can do is pray. I pray, and wait with diligence. I love that man with every viral load in my bloodstream. I love him like I love the Almighty himself. But no matter how much I love him reality sets in that he has indeed abandoned me. Love seems to have lost again.

I grab some clothes: a pair of bootleg cut jeans, black V-neck shirt, tweed gray and black pullover tunic sweater, and my Anne

Klein sports shoes that Xavier bought me from Bloomingdale's. I head for the bathroom to take a shower, and take my cell phone just in case my phone rings. While the water is running I stare in the mirror reminiscing about our relationship. I can't believe how time flew by. Actually I can't believe that Xavier stuck by my side. There I go again, knocking myself. Xavier always disliked when I did that. He'd say: "Speak highly of yourself or don't speak at all." I remained quiet after that comment because it made perfect sense to me. Why was I knocking myself in the first place? I guess because I looked at myself in a different light. Here I was unemployed. Anonymous was gone. I pretty much co-signed everything that meant anything to me for what…love. And in the end of it all I lost me, myself, and I in the process. And once you lose you there is nothing left to look forward to. Your whole perception of yourself changes. I don't even feel like me anymore because deep within I feel like a complete failure. This is a dose of reality medicine that I have a difficult time swallowing. It was not easy for me having a man wanting to provide for me. Oh, I'd never ask for a damn thing. I had too much pride. Too much. Hell, that's all I had left and you think that I was just going to hand that over too. I don't think so. I had no choice but to hold on to that and my dignity. Without either I might as well sell my soul to the devil because eventually he'd probably snatch me up when I least expected it anyway.

Age had a lot to do with the way Xavier treated me. He was as charismatic as they'd come. Him being older made me appreciate the qualities in which he held. He was refined. Compassionate. Adorable. He showed empathy. He was strong, resilient, and pure. It was refreshing to have someone who took the lead. Who showed he cared. He wasn't always the affectionate type of man. No, he seemed set in his ways. He could be somewhat of a tight ass at times. It seemed strange because once we would get out of our normal environment and go somewhere else where no one knew us he'd seem like a totally different man. He'd smile more. Laugh. Share his day. Tell me stories of his past life. He was touchy-feely with me too. He'd kiss me out in public. He just made me feel so damned loved. He was confident, less grumpy, and he was even fun to be around. He would even get on the dance floor and dance a two-step with me. Hold me so close to his heart and whisper in my ear how much he truly loved me. Yes, he could be very direct and sharp with his tongue, but I realized that there was a lot buried within him that he had not shared with the outside world. Often I felt in good hands but I also felt like there was something missing between us. Intimacy.

43

We had never crossed that line in the sex department and it kind of sort of bothered me, just a bit. Don't get me wrong I fully understood the magnitude of his discomfort. How difficult it might've been to even conceive of the thought of making love to someone infected. But I knew sooner or later it was bound to happen because we'd eventually be husband and wife. You have to understand it was inconceivable to me to have a man, any man, for that matter stick by me. And to have one say that he loved me seemed even more inconceivable but I knew in my heart of hearts that Xavier did. Not only did he speak it, he showed it with his actions. Not all of his actions were shown in a positive way, though. Sometimes he could be nasty toward me. And often I'd take it to save face, you know? Sometimes he'd get so irritated with me that he would completely shutdown.

I remember he had a cold or something related to a cold. His side and stomach and back and knees were bothering him too. I thought maybe he might've had a virus or the flu. I was always concerned when anything was wrong with him because Xavier did a lot for a man his age. I mean it seemed like he over did it at times. And that really concerned me, especially when he'd complain about all these little ailments that could potentially turn into bigger ailments. I was always afraid that something dreadful would happen to him and I wouldn't be prepared, you know. I was seriously paranoid, I'll admit. Xavier meant the world to me. And I never ever wanted to lose my world. Anyway, he called to say that he was dropping me off some money that day. January 8th. I'd never forget the date for as long as I live. We walked out to the hallway of the building I was staying in. I won't say living, as in a home, because it didn't feel like a home. It wasn't welcoming like a home. It felt more like a prison and I always felt like I was an inmate doing some serious time. I think the pressure of me being in my situation had a lot to do with his frustrations. Thinking back, yes, I can clearly see it now. Xavier was very outspoken when he wanted to be. He had many sides to him. This I'd come to find out the hard way.

"You look like I feel," Xavier said dressed in his gray sweats and chocolate brown jacket with a baseball cap on his head. His eyes told of how he felt inside…shitty. This burning in my stomach kept me on edge. I was hurting most of the day because I had so much on my heart. So much I needed to release before I popped. The last thing I wanted was to become my mother by having a nervous breakdown. I sighed, and then spoke in a delicate tone to him "I need to talk to you." A grimace appeared on his face like he was instantly annoyed with me. His eyes were set and glazed. I knew the look all too well but I disregarded it because I needed to free my soul so I took the plunge knowing that this would either break us or make us whole again.

I remember when I used to always bring up Travar to Xavier. We were sitting at this lounge called The Z-Bar in Englewood Cliffs off of Murray and Hawley Street and as we were having a drink over general conversation Xavier politely said that he wanted to say something to me once we left. When we got in his SUV he put the key in the ignition and then looked over at me sitting on the passenger side and said, "Listen, you talk about your friend Travar an awful lot." His tone was nice and mellow. "Um, well, I would appreciate it if you didn't. I don't want to hear about him while we are together." I respected him for speaking his mind. I agreed to stop since I knew how much it bothered him. I really wanted him to be a part of my life, you know? Well, when the time came for me to speak my mind, he had already transformed into a ferocious pit-bull. I began by saying, "Look, I know that you work with a lot of women and there is one in particular that you talk about almost every day." He immediately got irritated and bullets fired from his mouth. Now Headley was a plump chick that loved to get her eat on so you know she was rather big-boned. Now I didn't feel that she was a threat to me because I believed that my man loved me. It was the principle of the matter. Don't ask of me what you can't or won't do yourself. Well, immediately Xavier took offense. "There is nothing going on with me and Headley!" he snapped. First of all, I never said that there was. I never said that he was doing anything with her. All I said was that I would appreciate it if he didn't talk her up so much while we were together. I heard about her every single day. I mean c'mon. "Every week you got something new. It never fails, Avery! Don't get on the elevator with me!" Xavier snapped again, with his face contorted of utter annoyance.

Ding!

The elevator doors opened and we stepped inside. There were two female passengers on it so I remained quiet until we got off and in his SUV. As both of us got in his SUV and closed the door, I let it rip. "Why don't I have the same rights and freedom of speech as you? Why do I have to bear and grin and suck-it-up knowing that it is bothering me? How can you ask something of me and I give you no lip but you can't do the same for me? It's not fair. I'm 'bout tired of you and your double-standard bullshit." I exclaimed. "Listen, all I came to do was bring you some money. I don't wanna hear this

45

nonsense today." Xavier said as he turned his face toward the window to ignore me. I felt so disrespected by his actions. I figured something had to have happened before he arrived at the building and I just added flames to the fire that was already burning inside of him. "I need to talk, why can't you just listen to me?" My voice was raspy and filled with deep emotion, but he didn't seem to care. All of that "love shit" didn't mean shit to me. I kindly pushed that shit to the wayside. I mean Xavier was infuriated and I couldn't understand why because I never accused him of creeping or sleeping with the chick. First of all, he never gave me a chance to finish my sentence before he snapped at me. I know it was a lot to handle with my situation and all. I told him about my living conditions when he came back into my life. I told him about me being unemployed but how I was actively looking for work. He knew I had to attend a mandatory Work-First Program in order to keep the general assistance that I was receiving on a monthly basis. I had no other means of income other than the money he chose to give me on the side. But what he failed to realize was that it was never about the money. It was about the man. The money meant nothing to me, but the man meant the world to me.

I knew how to survive off of little of nothing or sacrifice until something promising came along. I had my pride, dignity, and self-respect and I was not about to compromise any of them for him. It took me too long to get to this place within myself. Too long. It became about respecting me as his woman and his potential wife. I felt devalued especially by his sharp tone. I tried to hold his hand; he'd snatch it away. I tried to explain myself the best way I could without making him feel like I was male bashing but nothing worked in my favor. He wasn't trying to hear a damn thing because he drew his own conclusions. And he wouldn't pull himself back to me to hear or even feel the hurt that I was experiencing right before his eyes. I felt helpless and hopeless all at the same time. And it showed. It showed because I broke down in tears in front of him. I didn't care and neither did he. He was solid as a rock, face stoic. "How can you tell me every waking day and night how much you love me when I'm sitting right beside you and you can't even stand to look at me right now?!" I felt the tears beckoning to fall. Crying was my only outlet. It was something I'd normally do when I was stressed and couldn't hold the weight of my pain any longer. I cried so sincerely to be heard but he dismissed my emotions and me as if I was a nobody. I can't tell you how it made me feel…desperately in need of an open ear, someone, anyone willing to listen to me because I was cracking by the minute, not hour, day, or week…the minute. What really pushed me over the edge was when he said, "Get out of my car!" I could not begin to explain how that made me feels. The only words to describe it were "broken in a million little pieces." This coming from a man I loved was the most hurtful thing I could have ever encountered. I thought when I had to get the key out of the mailbox everyday was humiliating. No. Xavier kicking me out of his car hurt more than that. Reason being is because I truly, truly loved him. It was so unexpected, harsh and abrupt. But it showed me a lot of what I had not seen in him. This was who he could be with no effort at all. It was no act. This was part of his makeup and quite frankly I didn't like that side of him because it was a side that held grudges and played that tit-for-tat bullshit. That was for children not a grown ass man. Look, you have to understand I was a fragile piece of art. I could easily break at any given time.

Xavier's reaction took me back to every man that had ever done me wrong, including Poppa. I felt like I wanted to vomit but I swallowed the acidic residue back down my throat. I completely lost my cool. The pain was so excruciatingly painful. I didn't know how to function. I felt totally dismissed at a time when I felt I needed to talk. Talk to the man who I loved and who claimed to have loved me back. He being my man and he refusing to listen to me told me a lot, too. I knew in my heart that this man didn't know what love was. How could he? It no longer mattered that he said the word "love." What mattered was that he felt the word. He didn't know how love truly felt and it was a wake-up call for me—one that I did not want to have to admit to myself but I had no choice but to.

January 9th. I moped around the house feeling empty, missing Xavier, and hoping that he missed me too. I stuck to my guns. I didn't cave in like I normally would've by calling him. I needed some type of confirmation that I meant something to him. And truthfully, I got nothing back on that day. It made me feel lousy. I couldn't eat or sleep or think about anything, except him.

January 10th. I got the same results back, nothing, but I didn't let it bring me down to the point where I stayed home. The little help I was getting from social services I needed to continue to get because things were beginning to look hopeful to me. What I mean is back in October, I had applied for Bergen County Housing Choice Voucher Program, which everyone in Paterson had done. I submitted in my application from the Herald newspaper not certain if my application would even make the list since they were only picking the first one thousand people.

By the end of October, I received a response back stating that I made the list. I can't tell you how grateful I was because things were pretty damned bleak. Then unexpectedly I received a response from Essex & Phoenix Mills apartments on November 20th but I never knew because it had gone to my P.O. Box, which stated that I was added to their list. Something kept telling me to reapply and I am so glad that I did. So it kinda made me wonder if Xavier was feeling a certain kind of way because now there was some hope at the door. I thought he would be thrilled but he didn't appear to be that thrilled. I burst out crying. Yes, it touched my spirit and I had to set my gratitude free. I loved Xavier and all I ever wanted was to make things easier on him. I didn't like seeing him stressed drinking Bacardi-8 and Vodka with a wedge of lemon because sometimes he just didn't know when to quit. That's when I began to feel like I was a burden.

By 9:07 p.m., I made one final call to Xavier. The phone rang several times but he never picked up. Beep!

"Hi, it's me, Avery. Well, this will be my final call. It's obvious that you don't want to talk to me. If I've hurt you in any way I truly apologize. Wow. I just want you to know that I love you. I've never stopped loving you. But I guess somewhere along the way I messed up. Well, take care of yourself.

Love"

I need closure for myself because Xavier isn't courageous enough to do it. He always said that I'd have to leave him; first, because he would never leave me, but, as you know that was a bunch of bullshit. The last heated discussion we had was about Headley and that really, really woke me the fuck up. He used that as his excuse to make an exit. But the way he went about it was cowardly. By him not picking up the phone showed me that he had slight feelings for me, but not enough to listen to my real voice crack over the phone. By him not replying to my emails said that he couldn't find the strength to deal with his truths and lies. Deep down I felt that there were many that were never fully disclosed. They say love is blind, but I wasn't fully blind. Some things you pretend not to see or feel or hear. A woman knows when there is a shift in the relationship but if the man is not bold enough to say that he is unhappy, that's on him. I voiced my opinion on many things that I felt rubbed me the wrong

48

way. No, I wasn't the "yes" woman. I had been her so long ago. I was the "I-ain't-takin'-no-mo'-shit-woman" and he couldn't handle my tone or slick tongue. He gotta understand that when I last saw *penis*, that mutha— rubbed me the wrong friggin' way and the end result is what you get…a new and improved, yet infected, Ms. Avery Love. I never lied to him. Never felt the need to. And plus, lying takes up too much energy. Since we had never been formally intimate I knew someone was gripping his inches. No, I was not living in denial. He's a man for goodness sakes! He has needs that have not been met by me! Often I wondered if Xavier was a ladies' man. I mean we shared about our past but I'm sure he left the juicy parts out. I know I did. I believe that it is okay to keep some of your personal life swept under a thick rug. Why tell him your life history if he didn't ask for it. And if he does, doesn't mean you have to dig deep to give him all the skeletons.

Xavier didn't appear to be a one-night stand type of guy to me, but what does a one-night stand type of guy look like. It's easy to decipher that with women. Women don't stand a chance in hell when it comes to a man reading our dick sheet. Automatically we are labeled by the way we conduct ourselves, dress, talk, and by how much makeup we paint on our faces. It's stupid, sounds stupid but that's how the world is. Looks matter. Size matters. Money matters. Whatever happened to just wanting to be in love and be loved? It's a doggy-dog world, you know? There are other things that I wondered about Xavier, too. Like if he ever had casual sex with women in cheap motels while his girlfriend was home waiting for him. Did he ever have sex without using a condom with a total stranger; those thoughts go through my head from time to time. Did he have a preference when it came to the woman he took to bed? Fat, short, skinny, tall, white, black, or did it even matter? Did he ever have regrets? Or make mistakes that he'd wished he didn't? Like I said there is so much I wonder about him and so much I do not know.

Back in the day, everyone was sleeping around because there weren't too many hang-ups, other than STDs. And depending upon which one you got there was always a pill to cure, except for herpes, which became your life partner.

Nowadays, things have changed tremendously. The older generations are contracting STDs more frequently than the younger generation. Married women are becoming infected with the virus from their husbands. Yeah, infidelity is running rampant. And *HIV in the City* is in the highs.

If it took voicing my opinion about some worker whom Xavier

claimed he was not interested in, why not grab your balls and man up and say, "I don't want you anymore, Avery. Just get outta my life!" Like I said only a coward hides behind his lies. It makes me wonder what was of truth. It must've been some truth to it for his reaction to be like this. Why would he blow up for nothing? Sure there was problem after problem after problem but I was open with him. I never stretched the truth. I never painted this pretty picture for him. I never doused sugar on my flesh wounds. I kept it real—kept it straightforward. It was quite possible that he may not have had an affair with Headley but quite possible with some other woman who didn't mind sucking his…oh, I don't want to think about it because it is only going to upset me more than I already am. Look, I've already aired out my dirty laundry and dudes are still trying to hang my ass out to dry.

It took time and a whole lot of convincing to believe that a man could love me. I mean my track record with men speaks for itself: Hypnotic, Bit-of-Honey, LoJac, Blu, Travar, and Zaelyn. Oh, and let's not forget Danell. I don't think I'd ever forget her.

Before Xavier, men didn't seem to want to tough it out with me. They'd leave me and expect me to fend for myself. And I was okay with that because back in the day I could hold my own. I never depended on a man. Oh, that was up until I met Brick Sumpton. But after him I wasn't about to start again. It felt damn good to have my own. My own apartment. My own bank account. My own space. My own car. My own sense of direction. My own self. I have already experienced how love could change a person from good to bad and bad to good. How love can manipulate and make one succumb to things they'd never even expect to do. How love can make one relinquish their worldly possessions for a man. How love can make a fool of one too. I think I am a pro at losing so many things that meant the world to me. That's what's so good about being an independent woman. As an independent woman you are the leader of your pact. You call the shots of your life. You do what your heart tells you to. But mostly you follow your instincts on a lot of the decisions you make. But then, here comes love swaggering down the street with his I-pod on and not a care in the world. All he wants to do is discombobulate all of the work you've done. Just that quickly love comes and screws-up all of your progress. And you sit back bewildered wondering why?

I must admit I was skeptical of Xavier in the beginning. I mean think about it. I was hurt by a man, which happened to be my own father. And still today, I am slowly healing from it. Xavier and I were like night and day. We had nothing in common other than the obvious: HIV. With him being a founder for the disease and me carrying the disease around in my body that might've been the very thing that brought us together, and it might've been the one thing that broke us apart.

I exhaust my mind. Finally, I say to myself, "I don't know what it is. Only Xavier knows the answers to my questions. Only he knows."

***

Saturday

It's morning. My eyes are swollen. My legs have stiffened up on me. I can't seem to get out of bed. My body is numb. My heart feels heavy. I can't seem to let go of Xavier. I cry for him every hour of the day. I ache for him. I dream of him every single day, since the day he vanished from my life. After all these years I am still madly in love with him. I don't understand what went wrong, but all I can think is that I did something to drive him away. Maybe I didn't show him that I loved him the same. Maybe he felt overwhelmed trying to take care of me by providing for me financially, feeding me, nurturing me, trying to spring me back to the woman he knew me to be after the damage that Hellman had done. Maybe he needed something that I didn't give him. But all he seemed to say to me is to love him, that that was all he needed and wanted. Was it all he needed? Was it all he wanted? Could I have done more?

I was immobile with three bullets lodged in me. I was fighting for my life as well as our love. Xavier kept me going. He kept me hoping to regain some sense of self. He gave me the strength to push myself over and over and over again. I wanted to be every woman for him. I wanted to make him happy, but time was not on my side. My life was in shambles. And I can't help but wonder did that have something to do with it too.

You can't begin to understand how much I am hurting. Love came into my life. I touched it, kissed it, and hugged it. I embraced it for the first time and without as much as a simple goodbye it faded from my life. All I need and want to know is why? What have I done this time?

I need to get some fresh air so I force myself to get out of the

51

house. Dwelling over Xavier is not going to bring him back nor is it going to help me. I need to keep my strength up along with my spirits.

My whole life seems turned upside down. I am just getting back to the woman I had been and let me tell you it is not easy. If not for Xavier I know I couldn't have come this far, and for that I am indebted to him, wherever he is.

The question that lingers is: Did I really love Hellman? I don't know why this popped in my head. I take a split second to ponder over the question and all I can come up with is no. I think I loved the idea of loving someone like me. Someone infected. I felt that Xavier deserved someone better than me. I devalued my self-worth because of my health status and that was so wrong of me. What's inside of my body does not define me as a person unless I let it. Well, I guess you can say I did just that because I settled for Hellman instead of following my heart. And let me tell you that settling shit beat the living HIV out of my dumb ass.

I walk into the kitchen and reach on top of the fridge for my meds, open the fridge and grab a bottle of spring water, untwist the cap, slip the pills in my mouth, and take a long swig of cold water down my throat. I leave half of the water in the bottle and open the fridge and place it on the top shelf for later. I go into my bedroom and grab some undergarments, walk into the bathroom and take a hot shower to ease this tension off. Usually a hot shower or a hot bath does the trick, at least it used to. After my shower I wrap a JC Penny oatmeal-colored oversized towel around me and go back into my bedroom and moisturize my body down with Nivea lotion. Open the top drawer and reach for my navy-blue tunic tweed sweater. Open the second drawer for a pair of thick wool dark blue socks and then walk over to the closet and reach for my denim jeans. I get dressed. I don't bother to put any makeup on; I actually don't feel like it today. Some days I like to look natural, just some days.

I walk back toward the closet and reach for my waist-length burnt orange wool peacoat, oversized rust leather bag, and keys and step out into the crisp air. The brown, amber, and pumpkin-colored leaves have already fallen from the trees. The sky is light gray, looks like rain today. I inhale the air and the smell reminds me of fresh baked bread Ma'am used to make on Sundays. I smirk. Missing my parents is still difficult for me to bear.

I stop at the bus terminal to catch the 171 to the Garden State Plaza mall. Boarding the bus I give the bus driver $2.35. I see that this older man with disheveled hair, hunched back dressed in dingy blue slacks, a navy-blue cardigan sweater that is infested with lint balls, and a stained white shirt has sat down but has dropped the contents in his plastic bag on the floor. As I am walking toward him I lean over and pick up the bag of bruised peaches and hand it to him. "Oh, thank you, my dear," he replies. I smirk, and sit down six rows on the right hand side. I gaze out of the window thinking back to how my life used to be. How I used to be. I can feel this sense of loss creeping up on me. I can also feel a chill from the ventilation above my head so I button up my jacket and then lean my head back against the seats firmness, close my eyes for what seems like a minute, and then open them with a fresh outlook on life. A fresh pair of eyes makes me see the world in a different frame of mind. Even though I know that much hasn't changed, just the thought of convincing myself that it has helps me in such a big way.

Once I arrive at the mall, I exit off the bus and simultaneously say, thank you, to the bus driver who wears his uniform shirt that displays that he has given nine years of excellent service to his patrons. For some reason it matters to me. And I don't know him or his name, but in life whether a friend or stranger shouldn't stop one from making that person feel validated.

I enter the mall and stop at California Pizza Kitchen to grab a bite to eat before doing my window-shopping. The host, an Asian-looking man with cropped jet-black hair and olive-skin, who looks to be in his early twenties greets me at the door, and he then escorts me to a table. Within a few minutes a waitress dressed in all black with long brunette hair pushed back in a ponytail, with flawless ivory skin greets me with a smile as I am skimming through the menu. I look up and gape into her beautiful cocoa-brown eyes as my eyes cut over and glance at her nametag that reads: Lynette. She looks like a Lynette too.

"Hi. What would you like to order ma'am?" she asks giving me her undivided attention.

"Well, I think I'll have the grilled chicken Caesar sandwich."

"And what side would you like: salad, soup…what would you like to drink?"

"Caesar salad and tea, ah…"

"We have peach, raspberry…"

"I'll have the peach, thanks."

"Sure." she reaches in for the menu, and then walks away.

It doesn't take Lynette long to come back with a glass of ice-cold peach tea.

"Here you go, ma'am. Your food will be out in about a minute or two."

"Thanks."

Finally, my food arrives. I must say it looks delicious. I enjoy my meal. Then wait for Lynette to bring me the check. She does as I take one last sip of ice tea. The check is for $14.96. I leave a tip and head out the door, but not before thanking the host for a pleasant stay. From there I head to the Border's bookstore to peruse through authors' minds. I'm sure their lives are a bit more interesting than mine.

***

Sunday afternoon

After washing and drying my clothes I decide to get out of Paterson for a while. So I hop on the 191-Transit bus heading for New York City. I arrive at Port Authority and head down the street stopping on West 37th to Gray's Papaya. I order the "Recession Special" which is two hot dogs with sauerkraut, mustard, and a 14 oz. drink. I ask for a Coke.

"$4.45," The brunette-haired man says dressed in a white T-shirt, white pants, and white apron. I hand the man a five-dollar bill and wait for my change and napkins. After eating, I head down the street and make a left onto West 34th Street, then cross the street onto West 33rd near Madison Square Garden and Borders bookstore. This African man greets me as I enter the bookstore. I say hello and head through the store and up the escalator to the restroom. Upstairs I see that they have a Seattle's Best Coffee. I bear to the left and continue on my maze to the ladies' room.

Once I enter the ladies' room I see that there is a line of three women: two white and one black. I have what feels like a piece of lint in my left eye so I say, "Are all of you waiting for the bathroom?" They all nod yes. "Well, I am not cutting but I need to rinse my eye out." I head over to the sink and turn the cold-water faucet on, lean over and rinse out my eye. Then before I exit out of the bathroom this obese woman with curly mousy-brown hair and pimpled ivory skin, wearing a black shawl comes out of one of the stalls and says, "Good luck," to the slender white woman who is next in line. I know exactly what she means because it is humming in this bathroom like someone let out a stink bomb. My god! I smelled it when I first walked in but I didn't want to make it so obvious by scrunching up my nose. Women can be sooooo nasty!

I exit the restroom and browse the second floor.

I browse the narrow aisles: Psychology, World History, Politics & Government, and Biography & Memoirs. I stop in the aisle of the Biography & Memoirs for some odd reason. I slowly scan the shelves for a title that catches my eyes. I pause, and then, reach for the book *Queen Pin* by Jemeker Thompson-Hairston and David Ritz. The first thing I do is turn over to the back cover: *"As I tell you this story, I'm not the person I was. The woman I'm about to describe no longer exists. She is a character from a different time and a different place. But there's no way around it; she is me and the story is mine. I have to own it."*

I pause, and inhale her words profoundly. Here I am lost and so are Teka and Jemeker. What is God trying to tell me? I turn to the front cover and open to the first page and let my eyes scan her words meticulously. I pause, when I see the name Anthony, the name of her son. My mind drifts back to Antwone. Immediately I feel a sense of sadness. I clear my throat and hold back the tears that are dying to come out and I continue to scan the shelves. I pause, again, and then stop when I read that she was incarcerated. Just the thought of being in prison reminds me of how I currently feel and felt. I feel like I'm imprisoned within myself. I close the book and place it back on the shelf. My eyes scan some more and then I pick up the book by Darius Strauss, *Half A Life*. Boy can I relate to those words. I turn the book over and read the back wording: *"Half A Life Ago, I Killed A Girl,"* all I can think about is how I can become whole because I feel dead inside. I place the book back on the shelf and head toward the escalator with a flustered mind.

I step onto the escalator and head downstairs to the first floor. I head out to exit Borders as a pale-skinned guy dressed in a striped charcoal gray and black shirt with a pair of faded skinny jeans on and cropped jet-black hair opens the door for me. I say thank you and step back out into the world watching a slew of people enjoy their day. I head down the steps about to cross the street when I nearly bump into this black girl with her head in the clouds dressed in a jean jacket, gray sweats, and dingy white sneakers. What I notice about her is that she has a book in her hand that explains why her head is up in the clouds, *Getting To Happy* (the sequel to *Waiting To Exhale*) by Terry McMillan. I stare her down, watching her walk as if she doesn't have a care in the friggin' world. Damn! It must be nice. Boy,

I wish I could be her just for a moment, I think to myself. Her expression says everything that I am not feeling. I'm nowhere's near happy, but I so want to be.

I cross the street now on Eighth Ave standing by a Hispanic street vendor. I can smell honey-roasted nuts. There is what seems like a million NYC taxi's congesting the streets, bellowing their horns. The M7 via 7Av via Columbus MTA NYC bus stops and a woman with a puffy Afro, jump off rocking some fierce fuchsia stilettos. Girrrrlfriend is strutting down the street in her runway walk, huh. I ain't mad at her. I make a right turn and stop at Garrett Popcorn Shops, which is one of the *O* lists Oprah favorite things. I walk in and purchase small buttery popcorn just to see if it's as good as Oprah claims. For two dollars and some change it better be.

Still on Eighth Ave, I catch the shuttle bus in front of Schnipper's Quality Kitchen across the street from Port Authority. I give the Hispanic man $5.50, and grab a seat in the back, away from everyone as my mind shifts gears thinking about what I would give if Xavier walked back into my life:

I'd give everything I don't have: peace of mind, good health, laughter, smiles, great sex, gourmet meals, fine wine, Jacuzzi, a house, car, bank account with money to burn, business, children, I would give him happiness and lots of it... And then I pause and ask myself, *"...and what would you give yourself,"* and instantly I draw a complete blank. I guess I hadn't thought that far ahead when it comes to me. How sad is that?

It's close to 3:46 p.m. I arrive back in Paterson and frown. I slowly walk up to Main Street heading for C.H. Martin to get some Sensesodyne toothpaste 'cause my teeth are so sensitive these days, my favorite Dove body wash, and some peppermint Listerine. Without looking I bump into Teka again. I grimace, and then suck my teeth. This can't be a coincidence, I think to myself. How come we keep meeting like this?

"Girl, we gotta stop meeting like this," Teka chuckles.

I don't find anything funny. I mean c'mon, Paterson ain't but so big.

"Where'd your sense of humor go?" she asks.

How does she know that I have a sense of humor? Who does she think she is another Sylvia Browne? Well, since she knows soooo much why doesn't she tell me where the hell Xavier is! If she knows soooo much tell me when my life will regain some peace! Shit, tell me when I'll hit the doggone lottery so that I can get the hell out of Jersey! Tell me that!

Teka being in my presence makes me want to slap this bitch. I have to reel myself back before I actually do it. Oh, she makes me sick to my stomach. Why? I don't know.

"I'll catch you later, Teka," I say dryly, hoping she doesn't follow me inside. I prefer to be alone with my self-pity party. Teka's sooooooo not invited.

As soon as I get home, I reach for my home phone and call Holy Name Medical Center again.

"Can you tell me if you admitted a Xavier Combs III?"

"What's the last name, again?" she asks.

"Combs III." I say, releasing a hollow sigh.

"Hold please?"

"Okay."

"Hello, ma'am, there's no one admitted by that name. Let me transfer you to emergency."

"Okay."

"Emergency!" This fast-talking woman answers excitedly.

"Hello. Can you tell me if you admitted a Xavier Combs III?"

"Combs, you said, right?"

"Yes ma'am."

"No ma'am."

"Okay, thanks."

After I get off the phone, I smack my forehead. I completely forgot to go pickup my refill of medication from Mr. Clyde's pharmacy. *I'll get it tomorrow*, I say to myself.

***

Friday evening while I am sitting in my living room, alone and feeling lonely, something unimaginable happened. My inner voice, yes Avona, persuades me to go into the bathroom and look myself in the mirror. I do. What I see is an attractive woman, tall and slender, with strong, low haircut, and cinnamon-colored skin. I have never seen myself this way before. I look at the reflection again. God blessed me...Avery. This small experience encourages me to look beyond my perceptions and allows me to judge what I see. I have avoided mirrors, in an effort to avoid the pain associated with my fate.

The next day, I call a friend of a friend I met years ago who happens to know a photographer to ask for a favor. Sometimes you have to swallow your pride when you are in need of someone's help. So I do.

I make an appointment and have professional pictures taken in his studio, which is also in his loft over on Market Street across from the New Jersey Transit garage. I submit them to IMG, a modeling agency in New York City. To my utter amazement, weeks later I receive a call from the agency wanting to meet me in person. I drop everything and go.

I sign a modeling contract. I became a model, am held in high esteem, and put on a pedestal for the world to see. I begin to believe that I am beautiful and since I belong to an accepted group for once in my life, start engaging in behavior that is not truly me. Hanging loose with the in-crowds, drinking, and partying until the break of dawn I am livin' as I have never lived before.

During one of my photo shoots I meet a gentleman named Stacy Blazman, 6'1", light-skinned with blue eyes, thin nose and lips with shoulder-length blonde dreadlocks and sparkling white teeth, who, seems to know people.

"You're a new face I haven't had the pleasure of seeing before." Stacy says, with all eyes absorbed in me.

I blush. I can't say I don't feel flattered because it's been a while since a man has looked at me.

"What's your name?" he asks.

"Avery…Avery Love." I say rather shyly.

"Well, Avery, if you need anything do not hesitate to ask me, okay. I can get you more exposure. I know people, got connections to important people who can broaden your career, if you're interested." He says standing strong and confident. His eye-to-eye contact memorizes me.

I, being new to the game, believe every word because he sounds so doggone convincing. And his stylish clothes speak a thousand times louder than his voice. He is the flashy type who enjoys impressing me by dropping hints about how wealthy he is. I was already into him when I first laid eyes on him. But to be honest, yes, I am intrigued mainly because of his flamboyant lifestyle. Come to think of it I never really asked him what exactly he does for a living. But I adore his personality. Stacy is real down-to-earth, not snooty like some well-off people. That is what lures me into wanting what he has.

Living in the fast lane, Stacy and I develop an intimate, personal relationship. And as we grow as friends, Stacy introduces me into the life of snorting cocaine. I have never felt the way it makes me feel. I feel good inside, invincible, and powerful. My career is blossoming and I am finally on top of the world. I am happy, but am I?

***

Two weeks later

Stacy's mighty grip squeezes my right arm cutting off the blood circulation. I can't fight him off. Not this time. I can't stop the demon inside of him. All I can do is nothing. Nothing, but take the ass whooping.

Tears burst from my brown eyes as he slams me to the hardwood floor in the living room. My narrow face plunges into the wood splitting my flesh. Blood spews out and splatters onto the floor and amber and brick red walls like an abstract painting. Stacy won't stop. It isn't enough blood, I guess. The pain feels like he punched me with all of his might, cracking my right cheekbone. He busted up my eyes. Inflammation in my lips looks like a bee has stung me. He pounds me with closed fists like a crazed maniac. Whack! Whack! Whack! Ferociously, he beats me down. Grabs me by my head and repeatedly bangs my head against the floor. He kicks me in the stomach making me cough up blood. He nearly burst my left eardrum.

Suddenly, the room becomes dark. Am I going blind, I ask myself? Stacy tries his very best to break me. He wants to kill me this July day. And psychologically he does. Emotionally he kills me. He breaks me down to nothingness.

My body feels lifeless as he pins me down, twist my left arm behind my back, while his right foot presses hard against my spine. What came over him? I mean we had just had sex not even a half an hour ago. He was so gentle, so loving as our naked bodies interlocked. What had I done this time? (Sighing) There are so many "this" times. When will it sink in that he may not be good for me? I like him, but not enough to die for him.

"Let me up, STACY!" I beg with fear and desperation intertwined in my tone. I am fearful that "this" time I might not see the light of day come tomorrow. Stacy has a bad temper. I never knew how mean-spirited he could be.

Of course, he wasn't like this in the beginning. Something or someone changed him over the years. Maybe life changed him. (Shrugging my shoulders), I can't say. Stacy hurries to leave. And I manage to crawl to my purse sitting on the coffee table in the living room. I pull the strap so that it can fall on the floor, and then slowly ease my bruised body across the floor like a snail as I stick my right

59

hand inside the bag and frantically search with my fingers for my cell phone. I press 9-1-1.

***

The following Friday

I spent seven days in Hopkins Hospital and Medical Center and now I am back in the comfort of my own home. I swear I can't believe how insensitive people can be. I mean I contacted my caseworker to inform her of what had happened to me and why I hadn't been attending Project Learn and the chick had the audacity to have an attitude. I mean I had a legitimate reason, all that bitch had to do was come and see me at the damn hospital, if she didn't believe me. Why would I lie?

My cell phone rings and I pull it out of my back pants pocket and answer it. "Hello?"

"I'm on my way." Stacy says.

I pull the phone away from my ear and just stare at it, in disbelief. What makes him think that I want to see him, I think to myself?

When Stacy arrives he looks delicious enough to eat right then and there. Dressed in a soft peach linen suit with leather white sandals has me purring in my panties. Damn, he looks fine, fine, fine!

We take a drive over to Harlem, New York, and have an exquisite dinner at Settepani Ristorante Mediterranean Cuisine (196 Lenox Ave, New York) enjoying the ambiance as well as the jazz entertainment. We indulge in a wonderful meal. I have the pleasure of eating oven roasted lamb chops with mustard sauce, served with a pear stuffed with mascarpone-gorgonzola-cheese. And Stacy has steak marinated in olive oil, rosemary and garlic served with homemade fried potatoes. The food is out of this world!

After our wonderful meal, we stroll through the lively streets holding hands, taking in the culture and scenery. We go to Magic Johnson's Theater to see *Black Swan*. And from there we drive over to 42nd Street and converse at the bar called 42nd. We have us a lovely, lovely time—one that I will treasure for always.

60

I feel myself drawn back to those girly feelings that are now woman feelings for me. The only thing is I don't know if I am truly ready to start a relationship. I mean things are happening so fast and without forewarning. I know I keep asking this same question but what is a girl to do when all this fineness stands before her?

"Avery, let's head over to Lincoln Center," Stacy says.

"Who's there?"

"Roy Hargrove." Stacy lifts up this promotional postcard that is lying on the bar and shows it to me.

I know I have a dumbfound look upon my face.

"Hargrove...Roy...the jazz musician." He looks at me like I'm some kind of sheltered child from Cambodia.

I shrug up my shoulders. "Sorry doesn't ring a bell." I say completely clueless.

"Well, come on."

We head back out into the lively streets of New York City. I must say the show Roy Hargrove put on makes me really appreciate jazz. It was never my thing before, but it becomes so after that first intimate introduction. After leaving out of Lincoln Center, my mind drifts thinking about Anonymous and having a career again. I really, really miss being financially independent.

On our drive back to Jersey, Stacy talks and I listen. I don't have much to talk about. My life isn't that interesting these days. And I think that really is beginning to bug me. I like meeting people, interesting people, and learning about their lives. I guess you can say I live vicariously through others. It is difficult to stay focus when you don't have a goal, hobby, or a spontaneous attitude. I've changed over the years. I'm nowhere's near the woman I used to be and truthfully, I miss her. I really, really, really miss her.

The next four days, I literally mope around the house. I don't have any desire to go to Project Learn today. I know I am subject to termination if I don't have good attendance, but I don't seem to care anymore. I am tired of Skills Tutor, Metrix, and any other form of self-teaching they are offering. I am sooooo tired of wasting my time. I can see if these classes were giving me college credits or something, but I'm not getting anything to benefit me other than a bogus printout certificate. The damn thing doesn't even have a seal on it to make it look legit. No one is going to accept that piece of shit certificate. If anything, they'd probably laugh in my face and tell me to get the hell out of their office wasting their damn time. Who wants to sit on their ass from 8:30 to 3:00 Monday-Thursday to get $140.00 and $200.00 in food stamps? Friday's I get to leave at 12:00 after

Life Skills, which I don't mind going to because I get to hear our instructor Mr. Benton, this tall, dark-skinned man talks about his life issues. Some things he talks about I can touch base on. Other things I'm completely oblivious of. Regardless, I still have to abide by the mandatory 35 hours a week to receive my benefits. I don't see this program helping me. I can't speak for anyone else, just myself. I feel like I'm just a number, a head count to receive my benefits, which isn't enough for me to accomplish anything. I can't do anything like this, I say to myself. Nothing! And it is really pissing me off! So I take it upon myself to help myself. Push myself in another direction. That's the old Avery I used to know. That go-getter chick! I love me some her!

Come Wednesday, I have a different attitude so I go to the Employment Service-One Stop on Broadway. While sitting in the overcrowded office I pick up a brochure while I am there, seeking any employment opportunities. The brochure reads: Passaic County Multi-skilled Healthcare Worker Training Initiative, so I call the (973) number to inquire about it. I speak with a young lady and inform her that I am interested in the phlebotomy training that they're offering. She asks me some questions: What's your name? Where do you live? Are you currently employed? What are you receiving TANF? What type of medical insurance do you have? Medicaid? Charity care? Private insurance? What's your social security number? I answer all of her questions candidly. "Someone will be contacting you as soon as another class is available. They will either call or send you out a letter," she tells me. And that is pretty much it. Within a month or two I do receive a letter in the mail inviting me to a group orientation session to go over the 5 modules the program is offering as a grant for eligible participants: Pharmacy Technician, Phlebotomy, Electronic Medical Records, Medical Coding, and Customer Service Training. Any student who completes multiple modules can possibly earn up to 15 credits towards an Associate's Degree in Health Science. It seems like a stretch, me being a phlebotomist and all, but I feel I have the capabilities to do it, so I go to the group orientation session at Passaic County Community College on Paulison Ave in Passaic, New Jersey.

I will admit while sitting in this large, spacious room with a group of potential students and faculty, I wonder if it will be difficult to learn phlebotomy, given the fact that I am a big ass baby when it comes to needles. How will I be able to draw blood, if I'm shaking like a friggin' leaf, petrified? How will I overcome many years of fear? The only way I know how to overcome my fear of elevators, escalators, and heights is to do all those things on an individual basis. The best way is to pace myself. I don't want to overwhelm myself and grow panic, possibly go into shock, you know, so I go to the mall and purposely ride the escalator. Go to a place of business and take the elevator. Go to a high-rise building and look out the window from the 34th floor and try my luck. I have to do these things in order to not be afraid. It is the only way for me to overcome my fears on a penniless budget.

The group orientation session is very informative. The instructors cover all bases. They speak about each module in descriptive tone. They speak about taking an Accuplacer test (essay, reading comprehension, and math) to see where the student is academically. You also have to have a background check done (paid by them), as well as a physical by your physician (paid by you), if you are interested in the phlebotomy training, so I am well aware of what is expected of me. After the orientation session is over we are asked to form a line and to give the date that we want to come back and take our Accuplacer test. I choose the following week, which is on a Friday at 9 a.m., sharp. Again I don't want to overwhelm myself. I mean I have been out of school for umpteen years so I really want to take baby steps to reach my goal.

Everyone is informed that based on their test results will determine which training they'll be eligible to receive. So say, I said I wanted to be a Pharmacy Technician, that testing requires being proficient in math as well as pre-algebra. I can't remember that last time I had pre-algebra so I know right off that that is not the training for me, and they will know it too. I rarely used math other than when I had my business and that was mostly adding and subtracting, some multiplication and division, nothing as complex as pre-algebra, so depending on how well I do on the Accuplacer will determine which module I'll be accepted to take. I'm sure they have refresher courses should I decide to explore another module. But I won't concern myself with that, my main objective is to do well on the test and pray that I am eligible for this grant so that I can get the heck out of this bullshit program. I can't take it anymore! If I had hair I'd be pulling it out that's how badly I want out.

Friday. I get up bright and early, take a shower, and get dressed in a pair of black khakis, black turtleneck and charcoal gray tunic jacket. I put a dab of makeup on. Go into the kitchenette and drink a strawberry Ensure because my stomach feels queasy. I have to put something on my stomach as I take my meds. I always get nervous when it comes to taking a test. This has nothing to do with me being

HIV-positive. I've been this way since grammar school. Ever since I knew what the heck "test" meant. I always feel like I'm about to pass out. I know it's ridiculous.

I rush out of the house toward downtown Paterson to catch the 74-transit bus to Passaic. When I arrive at the school, that queasy feeling is still there. I try to tell myself, Avery, it is just a test, but even I am not trying to hear it. I am a bundle of knots and nerves. I walk into the school and tell the gray-haired security guard what I am here for. This tall guy with dirty-blonde hair might be the maintenance man tells me where to go. I say thank you. Then I walk toward the office and I see a lady sitting in there alone dressed in a blazer and blouse with light skin and her black hair is styled in a doobie sitting at her desk, eyes engrossed in the computer screen.

"Excuse me, but I'm here for…"

"Oh, what is your name?" she asks in a Jamaican accent.

"Avery Love, ma'am."

"We'll be starting at 9:00," she tells me. "You can have a seat outside. I'll be out in a few to come and get you's."

"Okay. Thank you."

I walk back to the lobby area and take a seat. There are four other young women sitting there. All of us are quiet, until this one brunette breaks the ice by asking me a question. "What module are you taking?"

"Phlebotomy."

"Me, too." she says.

"Oh." I reply.

That's all of the energy I have in me to say is, oh. I have to save the rest for my test.

"Ladies' come with me," the light-skinned woman says. Everyone stands to their feet and form a line behind her. We enter a small room; the same room she was originally in and we all are placed at different terminals with space between us. I believe there are four of us, if I'm not mistaken. We enter our name, address, and social security numbers in the computer and proceed to the next step until we come to the part where the test will begin. We have 45 minutes to write 300-600 word essay based on whatever the computer tells us to comment on.

Oh boy, I think to myself. Watch I get a difficult subject. Already I am jinxing myself. I always do that. Stop that, Avery! I yell at myself in my head.

Breathe.

Scenario: Maya Angelou wrote her memoir: *I Know Why the*

Cage Bird Sings. If you were the cage bird why would you sing? And do you think it would be beneficial to others?

WHAT! I yell in my head. What kind of question is this! Is this a friggin' joke? Why does the cage bird sing?! Obviously the cage bird sings because she feels trapped, dummy! She is in a friggin' cage. Duh? C'mon. The cage bird sings because she is alone in a goddamn cage, silly! The cage bird sings because it is tired of crying all the damn time! What else is there for the damn cage bird to do? I go on and on and on until I find that I have over 600 words. I am just rambling with clear understanding, but rambling, nonetheless. I stop at 731 words, with still 27 minutes left. I have nothing left to say so I work my way back up to the top and check for any misspellings or grammatical errors. Then I click, Submit.

The rest of the test there is no time limit. Reading comprehension I always dreaded because it takes so long to read the doggone paragraphs. Most of the time I have to read it twice as I am glancing at the questions. Which one do I pick, I ask myself. Think! Think! Think! Yes, I'm in panic mode again. Sweat is trickling down the sides of my face. My armpits are getting moist. I feel like I'm about to fall any minute now. Just keel over on the floor screaming like a damn fool, "Call the paramedics!" and then fall into an unconscious state. But of course, I don't.

I try my best at the math; obviously my best is not good enough because I never make it to the prealgebra. The computer tells me that I have completed the test. Dang.

"Excuse me, ma'am, I'm done," I tell the instructor. Then I leave still sweating bullets, fully knowing that the test is over. It usually takes me some time to calm down. By the time I get home I should be okay.

The following week I receive a letter in the mail stating that I am eligible for Phlebotomy training. Accompanying the letter is a yellow envelope with forms in it stating that I have to get a physical done before I can be accepted into the class. There is also a form giving them permission to do a background check on me. The rest of the forms are for personal information that I can provide. Since I know that the class is based on first come, first service basis I am on my job the next day. If I have to stay in Project Learn "one mo' 'gain" (as Poppa used to say) I am going to scream!!!

I pick up my cell phone and make a quick call.

"Hello, Dr. Fulmore's office."

"Hi, Violet," I say.

"Avery! How have you been? I haven't seen you in a while,"

she says excitedly.

"I've been okay. Listen, I need to make an appointment to see Dr. Fulmore."

"Let me see if we have a vacancy this week," she tells me. "Hold on?"

"Okay."

"Avery, how soon do you need to be seen?"

"It's not a rush, but maybe sometime next week, would be good."

"Ah, ah, how about Thursday, at 10:00 a.m.?"

"That's fine, see you then."

"Have a great day!"

"You too."

After hanging up with Violet, my whole mindset changed. Thoughts quickly raced through my head, would I be accepted as a phlebotomist since I am HIV-positive? I know that it would be wrong of me not to divulge my health status. That would go against everything I stand for. I'm not trying to be underhanded, but I feel like whatever I pursue there always going to be a red flag dangling over my head. Okay, I get it! I have an incurable disease, but does that make me inhuman. I still have to survive, I'm still alive, and I still have air in my body so what am I supposed to do for means of support, huh? This is the shit that really frustrates me. I mean I have drive, ambition, and a go-getter attitude. I love working with people, inspiring others and the whole nine but I can't seem to get a break because of what I have flowing through my bloodstream. And people wonder why people who are infected don't share their status. Either way you look at it, I'm doomed from the get-go, so I might as well do what pleases me and deal with the outcome later.

I start my phlebotomy class on March 28th. Room A201 is now my home away from home, at least from 8:00 a.m., to 4:00 p.m., with lecturing from Mr. Ulner, the tall, blonde-haired man who looks to be in his late fifties, who is our Customer Service instructor. Even in the healthcare field excellent customer service is expected. I receive a certificate from that class, which will really look good on my résumé.

By April 4th, I start my phlebotomy class with two doctors: Dr. Aleh and Dr. Si, both are surgeons. Dr. Aleh stands about 5'10" oatmeal complexion with a baldhead. He dresses in slacks and button down dress shirts and black leather shoes. He told us that he came from Pakistan and that his family was dirt poor. Well, not exactly, he said, "broke ass poor" which basically means the same thing to me.

Dr. Aleh is really easygoing and I can tell that he loves teaching. You kinda know when someone loves something because they are dedicated to their passion. Dr. Aleh really shines like a bright light when he talks about the anatomy using all those big ass words like it is easy for a novice to pronounce.

Dr. Si is from Egypt. He has a beige complexion and wears wired-framed glasses. His brunette hair is receding. He has a stout frame and stands about 5'10", with a heavy accent. Often the students have to ask him to repeat himself if we don't grasp what he is saying the first time. And he does with no attitude. He's pretty easygoing too. But he's a stickler for lateness. Well, to a certain extent, I will say. Some things he lets slide. I guess it depends on the individual.

I am really excited about taking this class, you know learning something new, meeting new people, and finding my independence again. Currently there are eleven students. Dr. Aleh said the class previous had nineteen students, which was a handful and a bunch of chaos when it came to doing venipunctures (sticks), which are needles. But before doing the venipuncture we must review the test and ask the patient if he or she is allergic to latex. We ask the patient for his name and date of birth. Then we wash our hands and palpate (gently touch the skin to locate the vein) using our index finger to the area in which we are preparing to stick. We use a tourniquet to assist us in seeing the vein more visibly. Once we have located the vein, we remove the tourniquet because it is not supposed to be on no longer than a minute. We wipe the area with 70% isopropyl alcohol and allow it to air dry. We then, put the tourniquet back on and use either an ETS (evacuated tube system) or a winged infusion (butterfly), or hypodermic needle (syringe), but Dr. Aleh says we will be more than likely using butterflies in the hospitals. After we have punctured the vein and see blood in the hub, we remove the tourniquet, then remove the tube, apply a gauze to the area and ask the patient to apply pressure, while we invert the tube either 3 to 4 times, 5 times, or 8 times depending upon the color of its cap. We apply a Band-Aid to the area, and then discard the needle in the disposable red container. We label the tube. Thank the patient. Remove our gloves, wash our hands, and go to our next patient to begin the process all over again. We also learn about capillaries: hematocrit, blood smear, cholesterol and glucose testing. We use what is called a lancet to prick the middle and ring fingers for those types of tests.

Next Friday, we have our first test, which I hope to pass. My study habits are not what they used to be. Every day it seems our class is dwindling. I mean we started off with eleven students, but now we only have eight left, seven young women and one young man: Jemma, Nore, Yess, Constance, Enitta, Sabrina, Dennis and me.

Jemma is 5'5" tall, with crimson hair with freckles and a rotund figure. She loves her long nails. She's kinda loudmouthed but that just might be her nature. She's pretty good at giving sticks. You know she has a steady hand and all. She can be a little harsh when it comes to other people, but like I said it's probably her nature. She has three children and has been married forever. I guess her husband knows how to handle a woman like her. I mean he better after all these years. I think she's in her early twenties or mid-thirties.

Nore is the same height as me...5'11". If I'm not mistaken we are the tallest students in the class. Her hair is usually braided. She has small children, too, and a sixteen-year-old daughter she adores. She has high cheekbones that complement her brown sugar skin with big doe-eyes and pigeon toed feet. She never married and says that she doesn't want to. That's what she says but you never know what God has in store for her. I think she's in her mid-thirties.

Yess has long brunette hair, dreamy dark brown eyes which enhance her cream complexion and pouty lips. She stands about 5'4" or maybe 5'5". She has no children and doesn't intend on having any. She lives with her boyfriend in Passaic. I think she's in her early twenties.

Constance is dark-skinned with long auburn-colored hair. She is curvy and loves to wear makeup. She's a dainty type of young woman, refined and gorgeous to any man's eyes. She has a sweet disposition as well as a soft-spoken tone. She's very lady-like. And she pretty much gets along with everyone. She has no children. I think she's in her twenties too.

Enitta is a mother of three. She is in her early twenties. She stands about 5'3" with caramel-complexion, almond-shaped brown eyes, full lips, and medium frame. I think, I talk to her more than anyone in our class.

Sabrina stands about 5'3". She's the only student who is currently pregnant. She has two or three daughters, but I don't know if she is married or not. Her ivory-colored skin is flawless. She has that pregnant beauty. Ash-brown hair, petite frame, she sits in the back row by herself, quiet as a mouse.

Dennis is about 5'8", bald, honey-toned with great big eyes. He is the tardiest student in the class. And he's the only student that seems to take naps during Dr. Si's lectures. Sometimes he seems a bit flustered about the steps when doing his sticks in Dr. Aleh's class.

His attention span is short-lived, but so is mine. Sometimes I find myself drifting in thought about everything that I am currently going through. I find myself eager to write, but it ain't like I can just get up and walk out. Well, I can, but that wouldn't be such a good idea especially if I say I want to learn something new to possibly help me move forward in my life. I know that I already have enough challenges as it is, but this one might be the one to take me over the edge. I feel like I'm at a crossroad, and honestly I don't know how the outcome of this may pan out. I think that is what has me on edge—the not knowing part.

Anyway, Dennis seems kinda hard on himself, I mean I thought I was bad but he takes the cake by having fits when things don't go his way. Kinda reminds me of kindergarten. He really has fits, but he really needs to get a grip before considering this as a career choice. Dennis might need some anger management classes too before attempting to work in any healthcare facility. I think he has a child but I'm not sure. He might be married; again, I'm not sure. He doesn't really talk about his personal life, not that I am interested in knowing or anything like that.

As for me, well, I'm a hopeless case. Squeamish and needles don't mix. What have I gotten myself into, I ask myself pretty much every morning? Well, I'm not the quitting type but I think I might've bitten off more than I can chew. Why? Well, for one because I am suffering from sleep deprivation. I can't seem to relax like I used to. My neighbor, Mrs. Silva might have something to do with that though. I mean she's an elderly woman in her late sixties. She stands about 5'10", with cocoa-complexion and big brown eyes, sporting a baldhead, similar to mines. It doesn't seem like she has many visitors' either, family or friends. She seems like the loner-type. Most of the time when I do see her she is heading out the door. She's never gone for a long period of time. When she does return she usually has a few bags of groceries in her shopping cart. She seems harmless but behind closed doors, Mrs. Silva is a pistol. She has some serious, serious issues. I'd come to find that out when she broke me out of my sleep like three months ago, and since that night I haven't had a good night's sleep since. All I kept hearing was her voice cussing someone out. I didn't think she had anybody over that time of the morning. All she kept saying was "FUCK, dick!" Then she started howling some crazy sound I hadn't heard before. She kinda sounded like a coo-coo bird or something of the sort. I was like…what! I rose to my feet and sat at Sis staring at a picture of me on my screensaver, then played a CD trying to drown out her voice, but Mrs. Silva voice raised even higher and higher especially her coo-coos. I yanked the earplugs out of my ears, stood to my feet, and banged on my walls, hard, screaming for her to be quiet. I was trying to get her to shut the hell up. It was too early to be listening to her ranting. But she wouldn't stop. Nope. She kept on cussing and fussing like she had lost her damn mind. Then she turned her radio up high volume as well as her TV. My nostrils flared. I was heated. I kept banging on the walls, but she simply ignored me. And every since that day, things have not changed with Mrs. Silva. That's when I realized that she has more than a few screws loose. Yeah, either she was suffering from some type of mental illness or she was just fucking with me by having me think that she was crazy. But who would go to that extend to get their point across, I asked myself. I know that there are some people who play the role of "crazy" for an SSI check every month, but I didn't think Mrs. Silva would be one of those people. I just didn't think so. I was up all night listening to that woman talk about nonsense. It really gets under my skin, I tell you, because I have a test tomorrow.

Friday at 8:00 a.m., I take the test and fail miserably. Talk about hard on myself. I wanted to go home and whoop Mrs. Silva's ass! Oh, I cried like the world was coming to an end. It really affected me in a bad way. I was sooooo disappointed in myself because had I been getting the proper sleep I would've passed that test, no doubt in my mind. Dr. Aleh told me or rather the class that it wasn't such a big deal because it was preparing us for the national test. Yeah, that's the one we have better pass to get our certification. How I am going to pass these tests with this woman distracting my every thought, I wonder. I mean I try everything by going to the library, bookstore, café, park; nothing seems to be working in my favor because I ain't getting enough sleep to be able to retain anything. My brain is like mush. I have bags under my eyes and that really bothers me too. I look tired, feel drained and it really puts a lot of pressure on me just to make it to class every day. But I manage to at least go. Now do I really want to be there, yawing and whatnot, no, but I have to stick it out. I have to at least try, give it my all, as much all I can muster up. I can't see myself letting Mrs. Silva ruin my life. I just can't. But I tell you this that fat heifer is winning, thus far, and that makes me mad as hell.

On Monday's and Wednesday's I have clinical with Dr. Aleh from 11 a.m. to 6 p.m. And since I haven't been getting but two to three hours of sleep a day, my body is a body of nerves. When I do my sticks my hands shake like crazy and I can't seem to control it.

How the heck am I going to be a phlebotomist with shaky hands, huh? I swear if it ain't one thing it's another. It never fails when it comes to me. Never fails for Ms. Love, no matter how much I push myself something is always trying to get in my path. The devil just won't let up when it comes to me and I often wonder why. What do I have that is so valuable to him? It can only be my spirit.

Oh, and on top of that I had Enitta do my cholesterol test last week. She used a lancet to puncture the skin on my left hand (middle finger) and it read 201 mg (milligrams)/dl (deciliter) of blood. Just the other day I had Jemma do it on my right hand (ring finger) because I was curious to see if it had decreased. Oh, those two fingers are the best fingers to use when doing cholesterol or glucose testing because their tips are meatier than the other fingers. Well, to my surprise, as the numbers counted down I was confident that it was normal, but it read 213 mg/dl. Total cholesterol readings that are over 240 mg/dl are classified as "high". Anything between: 200-239 is borderline high, and total cholesterol reading under 200 is generally considered healthy. Dr. Aleh said that the reading is not from the day of the initial testing, but from 4 months ago. He said it could be something that I'm eating, wine that I love to drink, or even stress. Ding! Ding! Ding! It had to be stress because I'm not a fast-food eater like some people are. I drink wine in moderation. I'm not a lush of any sort so what's left, huh? STRESS!! And MRS. SILVA!! I know the normal body temperature is 98.6, but I know my body temperature was well above those numbers. The past few days I was a ball of roaring fire inside. I was beside myself. I tell you I want to go home, knock on Mrs. Silva's door, and tie her ass up and cover her mouth with duct tape until I take my test on Friday. That old biddy is stressing me out!

I have another test come next Friday, May 12th, and I hope I can focus enough to pass this one. If not, I think I should just call it a friggin' day and stick to what I know…writing, poetry, daydreaming, baking, cooking, and interior design.

Talk about off morning. Everything that could've gone wrong did. First, Mrs. Silva had me up all night as I couldn't help but listen to her ranting again. By the time I did shut my eyes it was 5:20 a.m. My alarm clock went off at 6:45 a.m., like clockwork, but I didn't hear it until 7:20 a.m. I had to be to class at 8:00 a.m., so I was rushing so as to not be late. I am completely out of breath once I arrive to room A201.

I sit down, exasperated. Dr. Si doesn't handout the test until around 8:15 a.m. I am on pins and needles again. It must've been by the grace of God for me to pass that test. It must've been.

Come the next week, I have another test on Thursday, and this one I have to pass because it pertains to what I will be doing as a phlebotomist. I have to know the Order of Draw (yellow, light-blue, red, red/gray (which has 5 names: speckled, tiger-top, serum separator tube, golden tube) green, lavender, and gray, what's inside the tube, and why is it used, and the most common tests it is used for as well as how many times to invert the tube once the blood has been drawn. Gauge size of needles, the bevel, shaft, and hub, and the differences between a hypodermic needle (syringe), winged infusion (butterfly), and ETS (evacuated tube system), along with a long list of other things. Yeah, it sounds like a lot that's because it is.

Thursday comes and I am a walking zombie. My eyes are heavy with bags shagging. I look a hot mess all because of you-know-who, yes, Mrs. Silva. I swear I wish I could just slip some pills in her coffee or something, but I don't go over to visit her because she gets on my damn nerves. It seems every time I have a friggin' test she acts like an idiot. I don't even bother to rush to class. Nope. I am dragging today. All I want to do is take this test and take my ass somewhere where I can rest my head. I am beyond tired. It's a shame that I have an apartment that I can't even go home to. What kind of sense does that make? Well, I guess it makes a lot of sense considering my situation. I don't want to snap and beat that old lady ass. So I best stay away from her, at least until I calm myself down.

Dr. Si's passes out the test at 8:30 a.m., and I try to strain my brain to remember. My mind seems to be dragging too. I take one deep breath and tell myself to do the best that I can. Don't sweat it, girl, I tell myself. Just do the best you can, no pressure. Yeah, okay, I think to myself. There are 50 questions, all multiple choices. Ok, which should I pick, I ask myself, after reading the question twice. Some answers come to me right away but others have my head hurting trying to figure out which one to pick. I say, screw it, just pick one, and be done with it. So I do.

I manage to complete my test within a half hour. I feel a little nervous. I hope I passed this one because if not I am most definitely calling it quits. There is no way I'm going to make it through with Mrs. Silva constantly disturbing my peace. Within fifteen minutes Dr. Si hands me back my test. I swear I am afraid to look, but I peep out of my right eye to see. And there it is in bright red ink an 88. I nearly fall to my feet. I am so relieved that I am still in the running to make it out of this class alive. Of course, my whole attitude changes I can't very well let Mrs. Silva win. No way, no how, will I let that old biddy win!

After we all take our tests, Dr. Si hands out our take home test for our final examine, which consists of 50 questions, all multiple choice. Dang! I nearly forgot that I have a term paper due about Bernard-Soulier Syndrome (hereditary platelet disorder), on Monday for Dr. Aleh's class. And then I have to start my clinical at Hopkins Hospital and Medical Center on the 31st. In June; I rotate to Hopkins Hospital Wayne General and while doing my clinical at both hospitals I also have to start studying to take my national test to become certified as a registered phlebotomist technician (RPT). Dr. Aleh says that the test will be 200 questions. I can barely do fifty, now I have to try to pass with 200, oh, boy. I tell you my plate is overflowing. I cannot afford to fail at this. I just can't. With everything that I've endured life has not been too kind to me but I've always prevailed through each and every circumstance that has come my way. I guess I have to look at this as another one of those circumstances. All I need right now is for Mrs. Silva to cut me some slack. That's wishful thinking, I think to myself. Mrs. Silva will continue to be a pain in my ass. This I know to be true, so I might as well roll with the punches because that damn woman is living in her own little world.

If I complain to the committee board I wonder if it will make a difference. What would they do to Mrs. Silva? I mean I wouldn't want her to get kicked out of her apartment or anything like that. All I'm asking for is some peace so that I can get some rest and get through school. Is that too much to ask for?

***

I have another memorable Friday evening date with Stacy in New York. As we are having a lovely time I suddenly realize that there is still a lot I don't know about him. And as we are heading back to New Jersey, Stacy voluntarily fills me in.

I find myself floating on his every word. His voice is smooth and mellow. He has a voice that one can listen to on an audiotape and not ever get tired of hearing it. It puts me in a relax mode. I am intrigued by his charisma, sense of direction as far as his dreams especially after finding out that he owns two upscale Spas—one in Upper Montclair, New Jersey, and the other in West Nyack, New York, called Whereabouts. He is my kind of man...ambitious, business-minded, and successful!

Upon me knowing this I feel a gnawing in the inner lining of my stomach. I mean here this wonderful man embodied me, yet the thought of possibly losing him due to my own selfishness seems rational to me. I convince that to my mind but not enough persuasion to my heart. Stacy has me hooked, lined, and sinking into him. I don't feel like I am drowning. I can't say with complete honesty if he has wooed me in so deep that I can't live without him. I ain't looking for a solid solution to keep him in my life. I mean what are the odds of Stacy and me bonding into more, possibly a committed relationship? C'mon. I can't see beyond my dreams, let alone this man. 'Ey the circumstances happened. We had hot sex. The thing that bothers me most is that I don't remember if it was protected sex. I think I had too much to drink. I know me though. I mean I would never ask for him to go raw with me. Look, I didn't do it with Grand, but I failed to tell him my status the night that we had consensual sex. Okay, okay, I was totally wrong for that. But if you recall I did admit my faults to him. No, no, it was not easy, but neither was it for him. I mean he pretty much did the same thing as me. Okay. We both were at fault. I never divulged my status to Stacy because I didn't think we would get this far. I figured dinner, a movie, maybe a few cocktails at D'Classico restaurant was as far as things would go, but obviously we are beyond that point. Obviously, we are. The fact that we were enjoying each other's company happened. So why, should I put every emphasis into believing that every thought, every emotion and hope—putting all of that into someone whom I never thought I'd ever meet? It just seems too good to be true. I mean my dream is my dream, no ifs, ands, or buts about that. And if he can't seem to wrap his head around it…then he can't. But in the end of it all it will still remain my dream. Whatever those dreams maybe…

Stacy seems like work to me. I don't think that I have the fight in me to even challenge him. I've been here before with Hellman, Xavier…love once whooped my ass. And quite frankly I am tired of getting my ass whooped. So I refrain from falling in a deep sea of love. I refuse to set myself up for disappointment or failure. I just refuse to do it again.

Once we arrive back at my place, I am exhausted. All I want to do is hit my bed. I look Stacy in his blue eyes and softly say, "You know, you really made me feel like a princess tonight. Thank you."

"That's because you are a princess. Next date I'm taking you to Mojo Black-owned Mediterranean Soul Food Restaurant on (Central Harlem-185 Saint Nicholas Ave, New York) and he reaches in and passionately kisses me so lusciously that I feel a flutter in my heart. I know this isn't good on my part. Stacy makes sure I get in safe and then he heads toward his SUV.

Stacy turns around before I shut the door and says, "You gonna be okay, right?"

I nod my head yes. "Good night," I say and then I shut the door.

I head for the kitchen for a beverage out of the fridge. I grab a Naked green machine and walk into the living room, sit in the recliner, and slowly nurse it down before heading for bed.

The next day, I don't hear from Stacy. That is when I realize he is gone as well as my five hundred dollars I had stashed in my panty drawer like a thief in the night.

Stacy

Lemme explain something to you about Stacy Blazman. I had to be reimbursed for showering that bitch like she was some fuckin' princess. Back in the day I had love for the ladies, but I'm a changed man. Okay. I played on Avery's emotions. Shoot me. I ain't the only nigga out here who has done that. C'mon. Let's be real here.

Look, it wasn't like she was gonna pay me for my time, energy, and dick. So I had no choice but to take back what was rightfully mine. Call it what you will. I don't give a fuck! You know something this reminds me of that two-bit-hoe...DeNetria. That skanky bitch!

***

It was a Tuesday afternoon. And I was getting my seventeen year old hustle on over on Dejavu Ave, when this crackhead approached me. Man, I couldn't see anyone trying to fuck wit' her. I mean she looked like shit.

"Yo', you got that?" she asked all fidgety. She could not stand still to save her life. Her eyes looked like two deep pockets and her eyeballs looked big as hell. Her face looked like a vacuum had sucked it in. Her teeth were discolored and rotted. Her skin was all blotchy and she had big sores on her cheeks and forehead. Her hair was matted and nappy. Her clothes were of a dirty yellow T-shirt, stained hot pink spandex with raggedy black flip-flops on her blistered and crusty feet. She might've been pretty back in the day, but today, she looked like she was on her last leg. Damn.

"Yo, you got that?" she said again.

I nodded my head. "Yeah, I got that."

She slipped me a twenty and I slipped her her lover. She stared at the crack vial and then she stared in my face for a few seconds.

"What the fuck you lookin' at, bitch?" I barked.

"You look like someone I know," she said.

"Yeah, a'ight."

"Nah, you look like my little boy," she said as her eyes began to water.

"Nah," I responded, swaying my head from side to side.

"Wrong dude."

I figured she'd get to steppin' but she stood there just staring me in the face.

"What bitch!" I snapped again.

Suddenly, tears slowly rolled down her face. "You don't know who I am, do you?" she asked in a crackling voice.

My forehead crumpled. "Nah, am I 'sposed to?"

"I'm your mom," she said in a faint tone.

Immediately a grimace formed on my face. "Get the fuck outta here, bitch. Talkin' 'bout you my mom 'n shit." I nixed her off with a wave of my right hand.

She just stood there staring at me. Then she looked down, opened her left balled fist, stared at the crack, and quickly walked off.

I could not believe my eyes or ears. *My mom is a crackhead.* I thought to myself. Nah. *I just sold crack to my mom.* I shook my head. Nah, nah, I wasn't trying to believe it. I looked nothing like her. Nothing. I couldn't say how old the crackhead was, but if she were my mom she would've been in her early forties by now. Damn. That crackhead looked busted.

Quickly I erased her from my mind and got back to business. At least I tried to, but the image of her haunted me. Suddenly a feeling of remorse came over me. I sold my mom crack. How do I know that she is my mom? That gut instinct, but I had to be sure. I figured the monkey would stay on her back so she'd be back for more. How could I forget my mom? I guess out of sight out of mind.

Around the first of the month that crackhead (who claimed to be *my* mom) came back. She looked worse than she did before. Damn. She had to be smokin' more than crack to look that fucked up.

She approached me doin' the two-step—all jittery. "Yo', you got that?" she asked.

I gave her my ass to kiss, then the hand gesture. "Hold up!"

"What? What? What?"

"Why you out here if you's 'sposed to be my mom anyway?" I asked her.

She couldn't or just wouldn't answer me. I sucked my teeth to get the piece of white me from the breast I ate from out of my front tooth that I had gotten from Hollywood Chicken and turned my nose up at her 'cause she smelled like straight butt.

"C'mon, son," she begged with desperation in her eyes.

"Bitch, I ain't your fuckin' son!" I snapped.

Her eyes were glossy and wide-eyed.

I swayed my hand in her face. "Won't you take yo crackhead ass home?"

"You don't tell me what to do. I'm the mom. You're 'sposed to have respect for your elders. Didn't my mother-in-law teach you anything?"

I massaged my lips. "Who's your mother-in-law?" I looked her dead in her glossy eyes waitin' to catch her in a bold-faced lie.

"Mrs. Rose."

I dropped my head feelin' like shit. She got me. Damn.

"Don't think I don't know my own son. I named you Stacy Blazman. Your DOB is…. I gave birth to you in Barnert Hospital at approximately 6:32 A.M. Your father's name is Pride Benjamin. You look like that sorry ass cracker. Ask your damn father why I ain't home. Ask him who got me like this. Then ask yourself."

"Nah, nah, you ain't gonna put your issues on me. You came to me, remember, not the other way around." I twisted my lips. "You wanted it and I sold it to you. This is business, not personal. You're the one wit' the drug problem, not me." I told her.

"You got that or what, nigga?"

I nodded my head. "Yeah, bitch, I got that."

"You ain't got no respect for your mother, do you?"

"You gotta give respect to get respect, bitch." I replied as I pulled out my stash and handed it to her. She in turn slapped that paper in my hand. If the bitch wanted to get high who was I to stand in her way? As far as I was concerned: once a crackhead, always a crackhead. I chuckled to myself. Then I heard that voice again. That goddamn Wino was back. "Man, why won't you stay dead, huh?" I asked a bit annoyed.

"You'd like that, wouldn't you? You still don't get it, do you?" That was your mom. Your Earth. How low can you go, nigga?" Wino said full of frustration and disappointment.

"'Ey it ain't all it's cracked up to be." I chuckled.

Wino snarled. *"That's funny, huh? Real funny I forgot to laugh."* He shook his head from side to side. *"You really ain't shit, you know that, right?"*

"Man, fuck you! You dirty bum."

Wino snapped back. *"I'd rather be a bum than to be a sorry-ass-good-for-nothin-nigga, any day."*

I waved my right hand to nix Wino off, "Man, go 'head wit' that bullshit."

"Aiight. You'll see." Wino smirked deviously.

"What's that 'sposed to mean?" I asked.

Silence.

***

Frederick, Maryland

"Do you see this shit, Asbury?" DeNetria snapped at her girl as she stood in her blue Lane Bryant jeans and a pink T-shirt and a pair of black flip-flops on, with her hair in tight spiral curls. Asbury was about 5'6" with blonde hair weave styled in a twisted hairdo, which accentuated her almond-shaped chestnut-brown eyes. She was dressed in a pair of old tattered jeans and a white T-shirt with a pair of navy-blue kicks on her wide feet. Asbury was a thick chick. Well, not exactly thick. She was a meaty girl like DeNetria.

DeNetria pointed her index finger across the street at this dude that surely resembled yours truly standing on the corner, downtown Maryland. She placed her hand on her wide hips and rocked her body making her titties jiggle with this mean look in her eyes. She was hurt. "Do you see this...!" DeNetria snapped again with her eyes gawking at me like a hawk. She twisted her lips with 'tude written all over them, and a look that was gonna rip her babies' daddy, which was yours truly head right off.

I saw Asbury and her standing across the street watching me, but I had a reputation to uphold. I couldn't let my boys' or that chick I was kickin' it wit' think that I was soft. Nah. That wasn't gonna fly. So what was a nigga to do? Do what I did best. Do Stacy.

At one point in DeNetria's life she had no more cares; no more worries because she figured the past was in the past. DeNetria wanted to bury all of her pain and start over, start fresh. But this particular day changed everything that her heart desired. DeNetria was fed up with me. She was ready to pump the brakes and call it quits on our so-called relationship. Taking a simple trip to the corner grocery store to get some Tostitos and dip for her Friday night book club led to this shit. She should've just popped that Jiffy Pop and called it a day, but she didn't. She just had to have those muthafuckin' Tostitos!

DeNetria repeatedly shook head as her curly tresses blew in the humid breeze making herself dizzy. She tapped her shoe against the hard concrete like she had a tick and quivered like she was about to black da fuck out. Why? Because I was 'sposed to be on my jay-o-bee. You know making that paper to provide for the family. A family, mind you I ain't ask for. Instead I was on the block wit' my boys' jus' chillin'. Pants sagging down like some teenager, drawers on display, wife beater T showing off all of my biceps and my mouth running a mile a minute talking to some skank-ass-bitch named Kindle Grimes. Damn, Kindle was a nice piece of ass. Shit, I couldn't resist.

"You gotta be fuckin' kidding me," DeNetria snapped again, eyes filled with burnt orange flames. She was in disbelief, feeling stupid as hell. She felt stupid for believing in me—believing that I would do right this time. Yeah. This time. How many times had it been? Yo, too many for her to count and for her so-called girl Asbury to listen to.

I don't believe he's out here again, DeNetria thought. Didn't he learn his lessons? She stomped her right foot, but this time nearly cracking the nail on her big toe. "I can't believe he's out here hustling instead of punching the clock at his job. He has a good job where mind you, he is 'sposed to be!" DeNetria snapped again. She snarled as she looked across the street watching yours truly get my Mack on.

That fool got me out here struggling! I can do badly all by myself. I don't need him bringing me down. DeNetria thought. She turned her head to Asbury and said, "I'm thinking his muthafuckin' ass is at work, not out here playing drug-dealer pimp." Asbury remained quiet not wanting to add more flames to the fire. She let DeNetria vent.

Highly upset DeNetria sucked her teeth, hard, and squinted her eyes, and broke out into a crazed laugh. Asbury just stared at her not certain what to say or do. All I could tell you was that a nigga was cold busted.

Anyway, by the time I arrived home, DeNetria had calmed down. Of course I denied it ever being me. That was another character defect. I was and still am a compulsive liar. And I'd do it with the straightness of face too. How you felt after didn't matter to me. It was about protecting me. Not you and not DeNetria.

I think over the years DeNetria began to realize that a nigga like me was not going to change. I didn't see anything wrong with me, so therefore, I couldn't change what I didn't see. I can't say that I didn't see the hurt in her eyes, because I did. But inside, her hurt could never breakthrough to the stone of my heart. Nah. I was too hard. And DeNetria was too soft. I needed and wanted me a chick with some backbone. Show me that you were strong in your position—

able to show a nigga that you know how to hold a nigga down when he is down on his luck. DeNetria was a weak link, so she got booted like the rest of the weak bitches.

***

I begin to feel bitterer and bitterer like my insides are about to erode. And I keep getting pissed because that fuckin' Wino won't back down. What the fuck does he want with me? Here he comes again, I say to myself. He swings with iron fists and a look of disdain outlining his scrawny face. *"You punk ass nigga!"* He snaps at me. *"Only a pussy would abandon his kid! Only a pussy would slap or beat a woman down like a dude! Only a pussy would cuss a woman out! Only a pussy would call a woman out her name...bitch, hoe, slut! Only a pussy would leave his kids in the dark! Only a pussy would have a woman tricking to fatten his pocket! Only a pussy would allow his woman to fall so far that she loses her kids to DYFS! Only a pussy would run from his responsibilities! Only a pussy would try to play a mother out to stop child support payments! Only a pussy would pay another man to fuck the woman he claims he's in love with! A love he claims he still can't get out of his system! Only a pussy would do things like that with a stoned heart of no regret! But a man..."*

Wino sounds just like a preacher instead of a drunk.

Wino starts bobbing and weaving and swinging harder and faster. He is a man of rage. *"Only a man would stand on his own two feet and take care of his legacy. His kids. Only a man would admit that he has twenty-one children, all boys, out in this world that don't even know their daddies name, let alone their daddy. Only a man would own up to his responsibilities and help elevate his woman. Only a man would apologize for the emotional distress he has burdened his baby mommas with. Only a man would cherish the fact that he was blessed to see fifty-something years old. Only a man would get out of his own way and seek his success and climb out of the gutter that his soul possesses. Only a man would reap his reward for his efforts, his struggles that have allowed him not only the endless possibilities, but also the known reality that he is worthy. To know that he is a strong, black man who has risen from the gutter and rose to his sole purpose as a leader...*

"Nigga, the only temptation for a man is the flesh of woman.

81

The visual is the bait. But the juice from her nectar is like an aphrodisiac that makes a man lose his goddamn mind. His weakness is the lust that she possesses. Whether innocent or erotic a man will battle in the boxing ring with his shadow to fight his temptations, but more often than not, the man will get knocked the fuck out by the first round because of the scent of a woman's pussy. A woman's aura will win mostly every time; especially with the one he has fallen head-over-heels in love with. The only thing a man can do is respect the love with this woman who holds the key to his heart.

"*And let me finish with this, just because a man is married does not mean the woman he married is his true soul mate. God made man and woman. And only He knows who is fit to be that man's queen. The heart never lies. Though the lies confess in shame. A true man will always accept accountability for his mistakes.*"

I lower my head. Run my fingers through my dreads. Yeah, only a true man. *I guess I hadn't arrived to be that true black man.* I think to myself. Something is still standing in my way. No. Someone. Wino. That drunken muthafucker won't let me be!

Frustration is brewing inside of me. *Why won't Wino rest in peace? Why is he haunting me? What had I done as a little boy to bring so much hell my way?* I pitch a bitch in my head. Then I calm myself down and ask, "Wino, what do you want from me, man?"

Silence.

Dead silence.

The bitch-ass don't wanna spit out no more philosophies my way. Wassup wit' that, I wonder. He doesn't bow down too long, though. Nah. He has to have the last word.

"*Negro puuuuuleasssseeeee. What you think the size of your dick makes a man?*" Pssssssssssssss. "*That don't make you a man. Nor does money define you as a man. A man defines himself based on integrity. He proves himself by his struggles and is rewarded with triumphs. You ain't nothing but a nigga. And in the eyes of the white man you will always be a nigger because you have black roots streaming through your blood! And in the eyes of the black man you will be identified as a nigga bitch. What do you want, nigga? What do you want, my nigga?*" Wino snickers.

I want to punch him dead in his face. I am heated—a body of hatred. I grit down on my teeth trying to cage the animosity that is stuck in my throat. I swallow it back down as it swarms around in my hot belly. What do I want? That is a good ass question. I have yet to find an answer to.

"*Stop pussyfooting around. You are really starting to get on my goddamn nerves, son."* Wino's voice is cutting in me like a sharp edged blade. *I'm tired of hearing you whine. Grow up! Own up! Stop bitching! Be a man. Well, since you can't seem to be a man I guess I gotta be one for you, huh?"* Wino says while he scratches his nappy head.

Silence.

Dead silence.

I grow frustrated by this dirty-ass muthafucka. "What the fuck you want from me, huh?" I ask again.

Wino punches his palm with a closed fist. Whack! *"I want you to listen, muthafucker! That's something you don't know how to do. Listen!!!!"*

Dear Beloved,

He was lanky, stood about six feet tall all covered in delicious dark skin. He was a poet, too. So he said he was. Though I never heard him recite any poetry. He also said he was a college professor teaching English at William Paterson University. I worked fulltime at Macy's as a Beauty Advisor.

He was peculiar, but mild. He was my left lung. And I was his right. We were inseparable. We didn't have any mutual friends and we didn't hang out in clubs or bars. No. We met in passing during a virgin shower.

It was a rainy day in March. I was getting soaking wet on Market Street standing in front of City Hall. He happened to walk by and saw that I didn't have an umbrella. It was that nippy rain too— the kind that chilled your bones. I was freezing. I only had on a T-shirt and a pair of dungarees. No sweater. No hat. He introduced himself dressed in a pair of tattered jeans, white button-down dress shirt cuffed up to his elbows, and a gray backpack about his shoulders with a pair of black converses on his big feet. His long locks were pulled back in a ponytail that dangled down his back. He looked neat and smelled like Downy. You know the fabric softener. I liked that.

He stopped and we engaged in small talk. Meaningless gibberish. It was innocent conversation. Nothing personal. "Hi." He said as he waved his massive hand in front of my eyes. He had an illuminating smile. It was bright like moonlight. I was daydreaming as he distracted me. "I'm..." I heard him say as he extended out his right hand. I reached out and our palms softly greeted. He smirked. "I couldn't help but notice that you are soaking wet. You can share my umbrella, if you'd like. I mean it's big enough for the two of us," he chuckled. It sounded like a roar of thunder. It sounded deep and strong and fearlessly sexy to my ears.

I introduced myself. "Nice to meet you, I'm Euphoria." I smiled so wide that he could see my tonsils. I remembered his face in passing. It looked soft, warm, and invitingly attractive. But what really captured me was the look in his dark brown eyes. His eyes took me somewhere. Somewhere I'd never been. I found myself taken aback by the look in his gorgeous eyes. I must say it was life changing.

So I took him up on his offer and shared his umbrella. It was purely innocent. Unbeknownst to me, it was the beginning of a life of sweet nothings and sinful pleasures. It happened once. Love came pouring down and took me under its spell. I was swimming, but not in blue waters, more like toxic waters. I didn't know. He never divulged. I never thought to ask. I never thought, yet I'm a poet. I couldn't see. Couldn't smell. Couldn't taste. It was like carbon monoxide—invisible before my eyes. But now I know. I know the truth.

My right hand wipes the steam off of the full-length mirror that's leant against the wall in the hallway bathroom making that squeaky-squeak sound that makes my teeth clench together like teeth crunching ice. It gives me the willies. My left hand grips the wooden cane that holds my thin body up. I sigh deeply. I stare at myself. Huh, ain't nothin' changed about me, I say. Contrary to what the outside world thinks, but nothing really to me. I'm still as vain as ever. Even though—.

I take a good hard look at myself. Blink. Blink. "Dang! You look awful, girl," I mumble with a grimace outlining my narrow lesion face. Blink. Blink. I look like walking death. I throw both of my bony arms up in the air nearly falling to my feet. Can't seem to keep my balance these days, you know. My shriveled up fingers quickly clench the cane handle. Ouch! That hurt. I continue to stare at my reflection. "What mo' do you want from my AIDS patient ass, huh?" I snap at the mirror. Tug at the tight skin on my puny arms—cup what used to be 34 C breasts—now are bite sized chocolate kisses. I do a full circle turn, and then stop to checkout my once apple-shaped ass that now looks like two flat ass pancakes. Where has my sexiness gone? I look like a dried-up prune.

Reality set in and I feel myself getting choked up. I drop the *cane and slowly I fall to my bony knees, tilt my head back feeling baby fine hairs brush against my upper back. Slowly I extend out my arms and spread my arthritis fingers with tears flooding my eyes and I snarl scolding him with such vengeance. You punk ass AIDS! I get it! You want it, don't you? All right...all right. I'm gonna give it to you.*

I grab the cane's handle, struggle to rise to my feet, and amble into the shared one-room wit' my roommate AIDS. Grab my black and white composition notebook and stretch out on the bed and open it staring at a blank page. I haven't managed to write a thing. Not one word. Consciously I guess I never thought you'd catch-up wit' me. You red-eyed muthafucker!

My spirits used to be high as a junkie, but then they fell as low as six-feet under. I straightened my mind not to dwell on the unchangeable. No need. The damage is done. I'm gonna take this opportunity and run like ecstasy in my mind. Climb that white horse and giddy up. I said it many times underneath my breath that I'd leave something behind, other than my name. Shultz, euphoria means extreme happiness. I can't say that I am extremely happy under these circumstances but I can say that I am a smidgen happy. I'm happy to be alive even when I feel death on my heels. Oh, I feel him like a hot-bloodied man creeping up on me feeding me that suave gift of gab. Talking about taking all of my pain and misery away. Saying he gonna make me feels good. Feels exhilarating and delicious pleasures. Sweep me off my feet like a king. Treat me like a queen. Take my soul to another world. I feels his presence most of the day and night. I feel his heat sweltering all around my body trying to melt my existence away. The heat is overwhelming, almost suffocating, but I manage by refilling that liter bottle wit' tap water and shove it in the fridge freezer out in the hallway to get nice and cold for me come those heat waves.

My jaundice eyes overshadows the satin brown pupils as I look down at the floor and notices the two-day-old newspaper sprawled open on the obituary page. This catches my eye. And in that moment I realize that I should write out my obituary. I don't mean no small talk. No. I'm gonna give it to you deep. Like it was given to me...long and deep. You gotta learn something from me, other than my name. Can't nobody say what I need to say, but me. Can't nobody say it the way it needs to be said, but me. Can't nobody, but Euphoria Drew Reilly. So I grab a pencil off the makeshift nightstand, which is a crate and I write these words:

85

*"If I Were A Sneaker I'd Pullback My Sole
And Invite Your Dumb Ass In."*

You see his love for me runs through my veins. It is killing me every day. I cannot get him out of my mind, body, or spirit. So, that's why I say: "If I Were A Sneaker I'd Pullback My Sole And Invite Your Dumb Ass In."

Yeah. I'd invite you in to take a peek of my reality, but you'd have to eventually leave and live out the rest of your life. That's what I'd do for you. I'd do it in a heartbeat just so that you won't have to endure what I'm enduring. I'm dying.

***

Wino scratches his throat a couple of times. His eyes look glossy. He blinks, and then his voice reduces to mellow and warm as if he drifted into another place and time. *"Her name was Euphoria. She was sweet as apple pie. I'd never forget her especially after she wrote me a letter. It wasn't just an ordinary love letter. Nah. It was deeper than that.*

"Euphoria. She looked innocent. Sweet. Untouched. I guess to me she looked pure. For some unknown reason I had to have her. I wanted to smell her. Taste her. Stroke her. Manipulate her mind. And slowly and meticulously I gained her trust.

"Euphoria was different. She looked at the world differently even though she was from where I was from. Her eyes saw something mine didn't. She had a head on her shoulders. She was a challenge for me because she wasn't toy material. Nah. She was like sunshine. Warm and endearing.

Wino drifts back to reality. *"That letter had power. It had poise that made a nigga bitch like myself breakdown. I fell to my knees and cried. But I still hadn't mourned the loss of love. Nah. Euphoria was heavy. She was too heavy for a brother and I didn't know how to handle everything that I was going through so I started drinking, gambling, and wasting away. I felt I had no purpose in this life. Maybe God might have something for a nigga to do—because no one was willing to give me a break. All I wanted was a break. A start. A chance. A purpose. I had none. And it broke me until I cracked. I became evil. I was envious of jokers who had more than me. What did I have? What was my legacy? What was I leaving behind?*

86

Nothing. Just like you."

"Man…get outta here wit' that bullshit! You fucked up and gave that bitch the virus, not me." I tell him.

Wino clenches his discolored teeth. *"Watch you mouth, Son. Don't you ever call Euphoria a bitch, you hear me? You still don't get it, do you? You still think that the world gives a damn about you. What are you doing to contribute to society? All you're doing is sucking up good air. You worthless muthafucker."*

I suck my teeth. "Oh, I know you ain't trying to preach. You didn't even have the decency to tell that bitch that you were sick."

Wino sneers. *"I done told you once, son. I ain't gonna tell you no mo'. Don't you ever come out your face calling my woman a bitch, again! That's one of your biggest problems you don't know how to respect women."*

"And *you* do! Hah. How many bitches have you slept with? How many? Do you even know? How many have you told that you had the virus, huh? I can't hear you. Those bitches gotta earn respect. Whatchu gonna do? You're dead, drunk ass nigga."

Wino cackles and slowly glides his dirty hands down his shabby overcoat to smooth out the wrinkles. His eyes are dark and voice is sharp as a razor. *"Yeah. I'm dead muthafucker. And so are you."*

"Nigga, get outta here wit' that bullshit. You buggin'. I don't even know why I entertain you."

"Oh, you're entertaining me, now, huh?"

"Yeah."

"We'll see who's entertaining who."

I give him a dirty look. "What's that 'sposed to mean?"

Silence.

"A wise man once told me: 'It takes a near-death experience to change a man.' Wino went on to say, *'Even though some men who think that they are hard can be softened by the barrel of a gun.'* I pondered over that for many days of my life. And then one evening while I was lying in this woman's bed it hit me. I was the gun that had killed Euphoria. Even though she died six month's after I received that letter I felt I had killed her six-month's earlier. Nah, actually, when she was first diagnosed"* Wino says in a voice of exasperation.

"One Sunday morning I was reading the newspaper and I just so happened to turn to the obituary section of the paper. And lo and behold staring back at me was a picture of Euphoria and the exact obituary she had written. I was overwhelmed with grief. She didn't deserve to die like that. But what killed me even more was that I

wasn't even courageous enough to be by her side. I felt I had brought enough mayhem in her life. It was best to stay as far away from her as possible. She never asked to see me and I never volunteered to be seen. She was withering away and so was I. Just not at a fast pace. God made me suffer. And boy, did I.

"Every day God reminded me of Euphoria through the eyes of other women. I saw her in my dreams. Nightmares. I saw resemblances of her in the streets. I smelled her body scent. Heard her voice constantly. Her laughter made me cringe. I had flashbacks of us making love that one time. I saw her smile, which was a picturesque of joy. And when I looked at my reflection in the mirror I saw her staring back at me, but not as I had remembered her. No. God made me look at what I had done to her. How she shriveled up into an old lady—a very sick old lady. Honestly, I couldn't stand the sight of what I'd done to her. Sweet Jesus. But what killed me even more than that was that Euphoria wasn't the only one. There were several who were unaware—several women who I manipulated to get into their beds—several women who had grown very fond of me. And several women hearts I had broken, deliberately. I was no different from you nigga. If anything, I was the worst nigga bitch of them all.

"Euphoria haunted me every day of my natural life, up until that day in November when I died. The very day I saw that nine-year old boy. The boy I told: "Nigga, you ain't shit!" I don't know what came over me that day, but God is destined to make right of my wrong. I'm a little rusty at this as you can hear. I guess that's why God took me under His wings to teach me a lesson. I believe God is using me to get through to you before its too late. But how do you get through to a boy who thinks he's a man? You keep haunting him until it finally spooks the shit outta him. Just as Euphoria had done to me."

"Nigga, what you want?" Wino asks. *"You still don't get it, do you?"*

"Get what?" I snap.

Wino throws both of his arms up in the air. *"After all I've tried to teach you."*

"Teach me, what?"

"All you had to do was surrender. Just give in and your life could've been spared. But no, you just couldn't bend. That street mentality put you here."

"I'm with *you*. We're here together." I say in utter panic.

"Nah."

"Whatchu mean… nah?"

"Look around you. What do you see, son?"

"The Gutter."

"Exactly. You never escaped. Even in death it followed you."

"Hold up! How can I make this right?" I plead.

"It's too late. Times up."

"Nah…nah. It can't be too late."

Wino just stands there with this smug look on his face.

"Look, I got things to do. People to see. Lives to embrace. I'ma father." I tell him.

Wino cackles out loud. *"So now you wanna be a father. Ain't that'a bitch. Typical nigga bitch."*

I crumple my forehead. "What's that 'sposed to mean?"

Wino sways his head from side to side as his bloodshot eyes pierce mine. *"I gave you so many opportunities before this day arrived and you wouldn't even as budge. Now that you're dead you want to make a difference in society. Typical. You're still selfish. You don't care about your kids—the mothers of your children. How you left them to fend for themselves. They needed you! Why weren't you there for them? Answer me!"*

I am flustered. I don't know exactly what to say or how to say it. My thoughts are scrambled. I don't have a reasonable explanation, other than to say; I just don't give a fuck. I am bitter. I am holding a grudge because of the man who abandoned me. My father. A man I have no relationship with. I always wondered if the man hated me. Did he hate having me as a son? Why did he leave? Why didn't he try to contact me? I felt this impulse to break something. But I was already dead. Can't bring a dead man back to life, can you? In a voice of reason I say, "Wino, I need another chance. Can you help a brother out?"

Wino taps his raggedy boot on his right foot. *"Why? Why should I help you? You haven't even acknowledged all your misdeeds. What about the woman who gave birth to you?"*

I am speechless by him putting me on the spot. But I have no choice but to answer him. "I get all that you were trying to get through to me. I get how important it is to be a man. How I should never deny the fact that I am a black man. I should be proud and teach my sons to reach their highest destiny—to know that their father will be there when they need him even if it's just to talk."

Wino squints his eyes. *"What about the woman who gave birth to you."* He repeats himself. I am trying my best to disregard his question. *She's a crackhead. She abandoned me! I had no remorse for her, none!* I think to myself. Wino narrow-eyes me. *"How do I* know that you are telling the truth? You ain't nothin' but a liar!" Wino says.

I crack. "Wino, you don't, but God does."

Wino sneers and nods his head. *"Oh, now you want to bring God into this, huh? God ain't got nothin' to do wit' this. This is on you. All you! C'mon!"* he snaps.

"Where're we going?" I ask with quivering lips.

"I'm taking you home."

"Home? Where's home?"

"It sure ain't where I live." Wino snickers.

My eyes nearly pop out their sockets. "Wait a minute. Wait a minute! Whoa! Hold up? Hold up, man? Wino, how can you bring a dead man back to life?"

Wino paces. *"Can't."*

"What you mean…can't?"

"Can't. What part of 'can't' don't you understand? Life is not to be played wit'. You can't bring a dead man back to life."

My bottom lip droops. "But, but on TV."

"That's TV, nigga. You were livin' in the real world."

"But so were you. Why did God bring you back?"

Wino clucks his tongue. *"He didn't."*

I look at him perplexed. "What do you mean?"

"You saw a reflection of me. A figment. You heard my voice in your head. You thought I was alive, but I've been dead for decades. And so have you." Wino stops pacing and stands directly in front of me. He put his grungy hands on my shoulders and takes a deep, deep breath. His eyes sink deep into me as they did when I was nine years old. I feel him. I feel something hurtful from his spirit.

"I'm old, nigga. I never had a purpose in that life. I was a drunk. A bum. I was the type of nigga who'd work just enough weeks to purposely get fired just to collect unemployment. Everyone looked down on me, including my own mother. She hated me. And she had good reason because I treated her like shit. God rest her soul. People didn't know my story or me. People just assumed that I was lazy. A no good nigga, they'd say. I had dreams muthafucka of becoming a writer. Black mans a writer. Ha! To my friends that was a sissy job. You ain't make no money being a writer. But I loved it. Yeah. But I let pussy get the better of me. I let it control me. Control my mind. Then one day, Death came a knocking on my door. Death knocked me down on my ass many times. Toying with my mind telling me that I had HIV. Telling me that I had AIDS. NIGGA, I was already dead in the eyes of my mother. She was my world and my world had long

90

shunned me. I was invisible. And I was ready to meet my Maker. Whether it was God or Satan I was ready. But He wasn't ready to meet me. I was ready to do some good. But He had me wait. I mean I gained patience. A great deal of patience. He was my God, not the other way around as I had thought. I waited and waited and waited. And then one day, God gave me the opportunity to help and mentor my Black sons. You don't know how that made me feels inside. It gave me a chance to salvage some dignity. Possibly right the wrongs of people I had hurt. I was eager to try just about anything to find closure. You see I was always hollow. But He changed my perceptions of my own life. The things that I've endured could've been prevented, but I had that don't-give-a-damn mentality. If only I had listened to that little voice that God kept sending my way. If only. But I didn't. I was thickheaded just like you. I thought I was a man, but I had a boy's mentality. Son, I killed a woman. Premeditated murder. I lived a life sentence within myself. She was a good woman who deserved a life. She deserved to dream, prosper, and grow old too. I took that from her. I did it! And it ate me up many a days and nights. I don't know how many times I tried to take myself out, probably about ten. Ten times, I tried to kill myself, but God always stepped in to intervene. I always wondered why. It never occurred to me that I had something to offer someone else.

"*Out there in those mean streets seldom, people stop to intervene. You get caught up in some dumb shit you are a dead man. It takes less than a second to blow your ass away. There goes another nigga dead and gone. There are choices. Everyone has one, but our people tend to procrastinate, make excuses, and blame the white man. But whom they should be blaming are themselves. Life is a bitch. And she "life" will struggle till the end. She'll give her all. She knows nothing in life is guaranteed. But she stands strong and tall in her position. If you want something out of life, son, you have to go out there and get it. There are no handouts from her. Do you want something, Son?*"

I nod my head up and down.

Wino cut his eyes at me, as his voice is calm and direct. "*What do you want, Son?*"

I find myself talking in my head to myself. *I am too far-gone— beyond any type of rehabilitation. Is there a 12-Step Program for dogging pussy out? I ain't a sex addict. That I know for sure. I am addicted to toying wit' bitches emotions. Breaking their spirits. Fucking wit' their heads. Having them bow down to my nigga. What is so wrong wit' that? They know the deal and yet they keep coming back. What am I to do? Nigga is drowning in pussy.*

Bitches worship my throne "Lubricated God". I have their minds twisted as well as my own. There is no way in hell God will spare my life especially when I'd betrayed and dishonored Him. How could I belittle the Man who had given me life? How could I even conceive of the thought of overpowering Him with what was between my legs? How could I disrespect Him in such a way?

I have long stopped loving me—stopped loving Him. And anything or anyone that came in close proximity of me. My spirit could never rest until I made peace with Him and then myself. With those whom I hurt, it was too late to face them.

I realize it takes a man to show a boy how to become a man. Since I wasn't fortunate enough to have a father I figured leaving a part of me behind would at least help boys who were fatherless. Help them understand the beauty of a woman—how to love a woman—how to respect a woman—how to elevate a woman—how to cherish the first woman who gave you life—how to honor the privilege of fatherhood—how to protect yourself from these diseases out here—how to love yourself.

I was ready to leave the past of me behind and find the true black man in me. I had to somehow deal with the resentment and anger. I had to face my fears, but mostly I have to learn how to forgive the one woman who broke my heart. That is like pulling teeth with me. No, it isn't easy to do. I have so much anger built up in me and I take it out on every woman. Why? Nigga. They are all addicted to my dick.

The only woman who stood up to me was my grandmother. I had never found a woman who wouldn't bow down to my bullshit. And it makes me feel powerful. That is up until Wino. And even though he is a spirit of some sort somehow he breaks through to the boy inside of me. But the boy inside is already damaged. And the man in me is already set in his ways. How can I change?

I hear Wino say, *"What you want, nigga?"*

Avery

A few months after being introduced to cocaine, Stacy leaves me for another model. I snort more in order to face the world each day without him. As soon as I leave a photo shoot, I head home to be with my angel dust, cocaine, or whatever I can buy from the unsavory characters I have allowed to enter into my life. As my wonderful, fairy-tale of a life spirals out of control, I go to Stacy for support.

He looks at me repulsively. "Look at you, Avery. You ain't nothin' but a junky." He, the wonderful, dream-come-true man who got me hooked, now considers me to be beneath him. I am devastated, but I am a junky. I crave cocaine. I do whatever it takes to keep that companion in my life. Things that Poppa and Ma'am or even Johnnie, for that matter would not have believed I was capable of, even if I had told them myself that it was true. I look like walking death, sunken face, big, glossy eyes, and a frame that only carries seventy to eighty pounds, soaking wet. Yeah, cocaine has me hooked. I don't see a way out. But then, someone Higher than me whispers in my ear and it shows me what could become of me. I see a funeral home, a makeshift casket, no crying faces, drunken pallbearers, and a crackhead for a minister, and a junkyard for a cemetery, and that shakes me up. It wakes me up so I seek out to get myself some help before it is too, too late.

My balance is wobbly as I head out of the bathroom stall and in front of the crystal clear mirror. I turn the cold-water faucet on and splash my face, three times, trying to wake myself up. (Sniff). Perk up, girl, I say to myself. Get it together. (Sniff. Sniff). I pull a dry paper towel from its holder and dab my face and toss it in the trash, but I miss and it falls on the floor. I leave it there and head out the exit door. (Sniff).

My head is spinning. Bright lights are everywhere. They are blinding me inside this studio. This place that makes plain Jane's walk out looking like superstars. I mean flawlessly stunning. A few touches of blush, eye shadow, liquid eyeliner, concealer, foundation, and lipstick and some gifted fingers can make anyone look like a movie star. I enjoy getting dolled up for the camera. Strike a pose, hold it, hold it, work it, girl. I laugh out loud. I absolutely love the glamour that comes with this fashion stuff. It is the highlight of modeling to me. Snap shooting for fashions extraordinaire. Wearing famous designers like: Valentino, L'wren Scott, Versace, Badgley Mischka, Jenny Paxton, Viktor & Rolf, Dolce and Gabbana, Oscar de la Renta, Armani Prive, Prada, Gucci, and Calvin Klein, and so many others. I'm thrilled to be able to honor their beautiful masterpieces in front of millions of fans that adore their clothing. This is the life for me.

I thrive to walk in the shoes of Alec Wek, Naomi Campbell, Iman, and even Grace Jones, of course on a smaller scale. I'm old. To see my face plastered on billboards like the Victoria's Secret models would be a thrill. I can see myself traveling to Paris and Italy, walking the streets of New York City hearing people whispering about me in the downtown area of Manhattan. Paparazzi taking snapshots of me at different locations and selling them to the tabloids and whatnot, I laugh out loud again.

Everyone keeps telling me that I have the look—that I can be another Wek or Campbell or even Banks. They say my eyes, high cheekbones, and long legs are things that I should cherish. They say that I have a look that can spot me new gigs like commercials or even a small part in a big upcoming movie. They say I have it, but in the back of my mind I question, what it is and do I really have it? Sometimes you have to ask yourself those questions because people will lie in a minute.

As I exit the bathroom door, to my surprise, Stacy is waiting, leaning against the brick wall. If he were waiting for me, that I can't say, but if I had to bet on it I would have to say no. I made my mind up to leave him alone. He's bad news for me. Look at the predicament I'm in. He could care less because we are through. I am a last week's leftovers as far as he's concerned. He likes to indulge in fresh meat week to week. I have pretty much lost interest in him. I gotta new man…cocaine.

"Avery!" I hear Stacy calling me but I try to ignore him. I gotta get home.

"Hold up!" he says.

It's not like I am walking fast or anything. I have on these six-inch heels that are a size too small. My head is spinning and my eyes are glossy and spacey. Everything before me looks blurry. My eyes expand in size just to see where the heck I am walking. I don't want to knock anything over. My breathing is erratic, too. My hands meet my chest. Am I having a heart attack?

"Yo, you feelin' a'ight?" Stacy asks. "You don't look so good, girl."

"I don't feel so good." I tell him, while patting for the wall to lean on.

"Lemme help you out," he says as if he is really concerned about me.

I know better.

"What did you do?" he asks, as if he doesn't know. "You musta got some bad shit."

Bad ain't the word. Before I can take another step I feel this rumbling sensation in my belly and then everything that I had eaten for lunch comes spewing out of my mouth, on me, and on these $865 tan leather (red bottoms) Louboutin shoes. I feel like I am about to pee on myself if I don't hurry back to the bathroom. I try to turn around to go back to the ladies' room but Stacy stands in front of me, blocking my way. I feel this sharp pain in my stomach and it makes me double over. I am light-headed too.

"Oh God!" I shout, while hugging my stomach.

"Avery, what is it!"

I don't know how to describe the feeling because I've never felt it before. *Why is he acting strange?* I think to myself. What's up? He's the one that told me to my face that I was a junky. Now all of a sudden, he's concerned. He's up to something. Maybe things didn't go well with those other models he was trying to get with. Right now I really don't care. I need to get to the bathroom.

"Move Stacy! I gotta go to the bathroom!" I snap.

He continues to stand in front of me blocking my way. "You need to go to the hospital."

Breathing erratically I say, "No, no, no…hospital." I mutter. "Take me home." I inhale. Exhale. "I'll be fine."

Gradually Stacy takes me by the forearm and guides me outside into the wintry air. The coldness slaps me in the face, hard. I start shivering and my eyes begin to water. I keep one foot in front of the other trying not to fall on my ass and break my neck. The walkway is slippery with black ice and chunks of hard, discolored snow. Stacy says, "Avery lean against the car so that I can open the door."

I stand wobbling.

"Aiight. Lemme help you in. Take your time." Stacy says.

I slide in the burgundy Thunderbird and sink my buttocks in his black leather seat. My body is shivering even more because the leather is cold. Stacy jumps in on the driver's side and puts his key in the ignition to get the car warm before he pulls off. He wraps his long, muscular arms around me to try to warm me up. My head continues to spin 'round and 'round. I feel like I want to puke again.

"Stacy, I gotta throw up." I manage to push the "down" button to the window, stick my head out, and puke my brains out.

He pulls off like a bat outta hell. I shut my eyes and the world in which I know it suddenly becomes indifferent.

JaVonna

After I sweat my hair out from fucking Christopher's brains out I head for our master bathroom and jump in the shower while he snores his heart out. That's when you know you done fucked a nigga good when the nigga falls fast asleep. I yawn, and then head to the bathroom in nothing but bare skin to take a hot shower. I cannot believe I am about to meet this boring ass man to see a boring ass play. What in the hell did Avery see in this old ass dude? I mean is he spontaneous, fun, are there any sparks between them? Xavier seems like a stickler to me. He seems like the kind of man who does not have a clue about how to woo a woman. A man who thinks passing off some money, taking me out probably every Friday evening for a cocktail and dinner is going to prove his love. I learned from experience that money does talk, but the heart speaks louder. A woman wants to be loved and if it so happens to be that her man has a pocket full of ducks, so be it. But if she had to choose, I bet your last dollar she'll pick a man to love her than a man who just wants to have a trophy on his arm and his name tattooed on the lips of her pussy.

Xavier gotta be in his late fifties or early sixties, at least. Men that age have a tendency to be duds. They don't wanna do shit but watch sports and play the pick-it, hoping to strike it rich and tell their pussy on the side how much they gonna do for her. Yeah…aiight. You know damn well you are lying because once you cash that muthafucking check your ass is gonna play fuckin' ghost and act like you ain't never laid eyes on her or her once-upon-a-time-good-ass-pussy. You will diss her in a heartbeat. I don't know why niggas can't seem to tell the truth. Just tell that bitch, "Listen; if I win the lottery I'm gonna leave your broke ass. Bottom-line. So you better stack your ducks away, just in case. Don't say I didn't warn you, okay." Just tell the truth. Why string someone along for nothing. The way I see it it makes it hard for the woman if she's much younger, outgoing, and a socialite dealing with an older man. Does he become a hindrance? If he is she won't ever tell, because, first of all, she is in love with him—either him or his swollen pockets. The last thing she wants to do is hurt her man's feeling or damage his ego. Now a woman like myself, I don't give a fuck. I'll tell a nigga in a minute: "Hell, no, I don't wanna go there! Every time I get in this damn car, ain't even get my ass imprint in the seat yet, you're asking me where I wanna go! Don't you have a mind of your own? Can't you make a decision and stick with it. Surprise a bitch sometimes! Is it gonna hurt you to use that brain of yours, huh?" See that's how I get down. I don't have time to be trying to pacify a man that will probably only leave me anyway.

Well, I can sit here and wonder or go and find out. I blow dry my hair and set it in hot curlers while putting my makeup on. I already have an idea of what I'll be wearing this evening, Dolce & Gabbana black dress, Prada boots, and my black goose down with black leather gloves. I don't normally wear hats because I hate to get my hair messed-up.

After I get dazzling, I give Christopher a peck on the cheek and head out the door. As soon as I step foot outside I say to myself, it is cold as hell out here. And I got the nerve to have on a short mini-skirt with tights. I rush to get into my car and turn the heat up knowing that it is going to take a few minutes for the car to warm up. I rub my hands together and blow warm air in my palms to keep my hands from becoming numb. I wait about ten minutes before pulling off. Once I'm all toasty I slip in my CD and start lip singing to Jill Scott, "Livin' my life like its golden…" I know that's right, I say to myself, excitedly.

The drive to Englewood takes less than twenty minutes. I drive around trying to find a parking space or lot. Once I uncover one, I park, and before I exit out of the car I call Xavier, "Hi, I'm here. I'm getting out of the car now. See you in a minute."

I watch each step I take making sure I don't bust my ass in these eight-inch boots toward Bergen PAC.

As I am walking up the street I see a man walking toward me dressed in a pair of tan corduroys, turtleneck, and chocolate brown three-quarter length sheep skin coat with his hands in his pockets and a sheep skin hat to match and some dark brown ankle boots.

I wave.

Xavier smiles.

He greets me by giving me a gentle kiss on the cheek.

"Glad you could make it," Xavier says in his baritone voice.

I smile with my eyes. "Baby, I wouldn't miss seeing you for the world." I say, laying it on thick as molasses. What I really want to say is, I could be home laid up in bed with my man but…

Look every man wants to feel special, appreciated just like us women. No, it doesn't hurt to boost up his ego, even at the expense, of telling a little white lie. Men do it all the time.

Bergen PAC has a better turn out than I thought it would. The play: *Diary of Shattered Dreams* is a story of persistence for Dream Fairmont. Her desire to become a playwright, producer, director, and filmmaker is an honest display of hunger and passion. The trials and tribulations she endured were one that really inspired me. Yeah me... JaVonna. It was also interesting because the narrator was none other than Mr. Ted Williams (from Homeless to Hollywood. The man with the Golden Voice.) How did he pulled that off, I wonder, because I thought Mr. Williams was 'sposed to be in rehab.

I turn to Xavier as we are in the lobby of Bergen PAC and say, "I had a lovely time."

"What are you leaving me already? The night is still young. Why don't we have dinner? It will give us a chance to catch up, get to know one another."

I glance at my Tiffany & Co. wristwatch weighing out if I really want to entertain this nitwit or go home and crawl in bed with my man. "Okay, why not." I say, with a hint of enthusiasm.

"Do you want to drive or would you rather I drive and you leave your car here?"

"Ah, how about I follow you." I say.

"Okay. Let me walk you to your car."

We walk and chat a little.

"Here she is." I say. Xavier takes my keys and unlocks the driver's side door and I climb in. I unlock the passenger side for him to get in. "Where are you parked?" I ask him.

"Just around the corner," he says.

I make a right and Xavier points out his Range Rover.

I pull up next to his SUV, he gets out, and I wait for him to pull out so that I can follow him to the restaurant. As I am driving I start weighing out the pros and cons dealing with Xavier. I mean he is most definitely a gentleman. It's just he's not my preference. For one, he is too damn polite. I like a roughneck once in a while. He opens the door for me. I like to open my own door. He reaches for my coat and wants to help me put it on. Man, I can do it myself; I mean I've been doing it all these years with no problem. He's a bit too reserved for me. I wonder if he ever gets angry or cuss likes a sailor. Does he ever do something out of his character? Believe it or not Xavier is really getting on my last nerve. Why? He's a dud. A flake. A bore. I need energy, sleaze, gossip, give me something juicy to bite into, you know what I'm sayin'. He's too by the book for a chick like me. I'm skanky, a scandalous bitch who gets off on controversy. *Please say something smart at dinner so that I can*

99

black da fuck out on you, I think to myself. I'm about to go crazy if I don't get any drama. I know it sounds stupid but you can't very well expect me to change overnight. JaVonna Banks is a woman with many layers. I wonder if Xavier will be able to handle a woman like me. I smirk devilishly.

When we arrive at Vybe Tavern & Restaurant on Vanderbilt Street, we park side by side in the parking lot. Xavier gets out of his SUV first, and comes over to open my door for me. I smile, but deep down I wish he'd get a clue. We enter the restaurant and are greeted by the host dressed in a tuxedo getup, looking dapper with freshly shined black shoes to match his attire. The host grabs two menus and places them under his left armpit while escorting us to our table. We sit in a booth with soft leather seats. While seated in front of Xavier my eyes scan the place. It is absolutely gorgeous. The beautiful colors of purple, red, orange, lime green makes it feel lively. The ambiance is to die for. Okay, okay, he has excellent taste. I'll give him one brownie point for this.

Within a few seconds the waiter greets us dressed in black trousers, white button down dress shirt with black tie and his jet-black hair is pulled back in a tight, slick back ponytail. The light glows on his olive-colored skin. He speaks broken English, but who cares this dude is hot. Tall, muscular, and packing down below, oh, I can tell.

"Hi, my name is Pedro. I'll be your waiter for this evening," he says, chopping up each word, except his name. He says it so pleasantly that I am really impressed. Most of the time I'm so used to Christopher and I going out to dinner and having to deal with grumpy waitresses and waiters who seem to hate their job but expect a fat tip. My tip is always the same whether male or female: "Bitch, kiss my ass!"

"Sir, may I take your order?" Pedro asks.

Xavier looks at me and asks, "Do you mind if I do the honors?"

"Not at all." I say.

"First, Pedro, we'll, have the New Zealand Baby Clams for our appetizer. For our main course we'll have two Black Angus T-bone steaks with potatoes and vegetables with a pitcher of red Sangria."

Sounds good to me, I say to myself.

After Pedro walks off Xavier gazes into my eyes. "So JaVonna, tell me something about yourself?" Xavier gets comfortable in his seat.

The first thing that pops in my head and spews out of my mouth is, "I'm damaged goods." How you like me now? Underneath all this beauty is a ruined woman. I kinda shock myself.

Xavier eyelashes flutter like he is caught completely off guard with my honesty. I take it he isn't prepared for this type of conversation. I mean c'mon, most women try to boost themselves up to be more than what they are. Me, huh, I don't know how to do that so I keep it simple and raw. This way he knows from the door that I got baggage and mad bullshit. He knows that I am a lot to handle. Now if he can hang fine, and if not, fine too, because I got a man at home who can hang with the best of 'em. See my perceptions of life have changed since the death of my mom. I take nothing for granted, but I do have a major problem with holding grudges. I just can't seem to shake that part of me off. If I don't try to get back at someone who has done me wrong I feel like the other person is one up on me. Like they have more control than I do. That gets under my skin. I gotta do something to retaliate or I feel defeated. The satisfaction is winning and I will stoop to any level to win, even if it means being alone or even six-feet under. Yeah, I know. I got mad issues.

Xavier surprises me when he reaches in and touches my hand. The feel of his smooth hand upon mine makes me feel a slight tingle in between my legs. Yeah, just by his touch. I cannot believe that he is this sensitive of a man. I must say it is rather refreshing to see. I mean this chivalry shit is quite intriguing to me. I cut my eyes over at him. *Hmmm? Maybe I underestimated him? Maybe, just maybe, I have,* I think to myself.

I find myself playing footsy with Xavier's pants leg. Up and down I slowly stroke his calves. He gazes in my eyes. I feel this heat surging inside of me. I'm on fire. I take another sip of Sangria, as does he. We stare at each other, and then I suggest that we leave to have some privacy. As we head to Xavier's SUV I see that he is checking his pockets.

"I seem to have misplaced my keys," Xavier chuckles loudly.

"Well, maybe there in the restaurant. Let me go check," I say. I head back inside of the restaurant with a little more pep in my step. I mean I feel slightly lightheaded, but good. "Excuse me, Pedro; did you happen to see some keys lying on the table?" He goes to take a look for me, while I stand patiently waiting for his return. "No, ma'am, there aren't any missing keys there." he says, in broken English. "Okay, thank you." I head back out to the parking lot. Xavier is leaning on his SUV with this huge smile on his face. He is beyond tipsy. I throw my arms up as I approach him and say, "Sorry, baby, your keys aren't in there. Do you happen to have a spare at home?" He takes a minute to respond to me, "Yes. I guess this is your lucky day, huh?" I give him a funny look. "What do you mean," I ask him. "It's your lucky day means you get to take me home and put me to bed." He smiles even wider. I can't believe he has just made my job much easier. I smirk.

We enter my car and as I am about to put the car in reverse Xavier whispers sweet nothings in my ear, which only stimulates every vessel in my feverish body. Instantly my nipples harden. He unzips his pants and pulls out his thick member. He grips it with his right hand, and then sl-owly strokes it. I exhale, somewhat in disbelief. I never thought Xavier to be this spontaneous. My body grows hotter and hotter. Damn, I can't even concentrate on the directions that he is giving me to get him home. All I want to do at this point is get my fuck on. I hope that Sangria doesn't wear off.

As I am driving I stare in the side mirror trying to distract my thoughts but I can't help but glance at her long legs. I take the liberty of pulling over and asking her her name.

"Eerie (no last name, just Eerie)," she replies in the sweetest Haitian accent I've ever heard. Eerie is dressed in a Coogi sweater dress with four-inch hot pink stiletto boots all covered in deep, dark chocolate skin. I turn and look at her with those cat eyes. Damn, I feel myself getting hotter. Xavier is snoring lent back in the passenger seat. I try to wake him. "Xavier, Xavier, honey, wake up. I want to introduce you to a friend of mine, Eerie." I tell him. He seems so disoriented, yet his manages to open his eyes. "Listen, baby, um, how about all three of us hang out, what you think?" I ask him. Xavier nods his head yes. That Sangria has really done a number on his ass.

It takes us less than a half hour to get to his home in Teaneck. Xavier opens the passenger side door with his fly wide open. He staggers to his front door, kneels down, slightly leans over to lift the edge of the mat to retrieve keys. Eerie and I stand behind him checking out his ass.

As we enter the spacious house, it feels cozy to me. "Where's the bedroom," I ask him. "Upstairs," he slurs out. He reaches for my hand as well as Eerie's. "Take us there." I tell him. Xavier leads the way. Each step I feel the lips to my pussy slip and slide against the wetness of my flesh. Once inside of his spacious master bedroom I glance around the room. So this is where Avery got shot, huh? I think to myself. I lure Xavier in by pulling my black dress over my head. I stand before him in a matching lavender panty and bra set. I slowly remove my tights, exposing my freshly pedicure toes. Eerie undresses too. Xavier begins to remove his clothing too. We kiss, not tastefully. We kiss seductively like two horny people ready to get their fuck on. I pull out my tongue and seductively walk over to Eerie and stick it in her mouth. We tongue kiss, wildly, and then Eerie pulls out her wet tongue and stick it in Xavier's mouth. While they are indulging in each other I remove my panties and bra, exposing all of my assets for him to see. Slowly his lukewarm hand reaches over and makes its way in between my hot thighs. He then gently strokes his middle finger inside of my pussy and then exits fondling my clit, teasing me by dipping inward and outward of my drizzling hole. As he is doing this, Eerie kneels on her knees and starts sucking his dick, while I caress her small tits. My pussy is sloppy wet as I kneel on my knees and softly peck the head of Xavier's bulging dick. I open my mouth as wide as it can stretch, elongate my neck, jerking it up and down as I twirl my moist tongue around and around, up and down, down and up, and deep-throat him, while Eerie gets on the bed with her ass raised mid-air ready to take it doggy-style. My sodden tongue slithers down to his pinkish testicles and gently swallows them whole. It drives him crazy! He squints his eyes and softly moans, "Ah, suck it, ba-byyyy!"

My pussy is blazingly hot. I mean s-w-e-l-t-e-r-ing. Pussy juice is dripping from my fleshy folds onto the plush camel-colored carpet. Xavier lifts me up and carries me to the king-sized bed and lays me down, as he sticks his dick in Eerie's sexy ass. After pleasuring her, he takes his time to lie on top of me and we tongue kiss, wildly. I close my eyes. "Open your eyes, J," he says with authority. "I want to look into your eyes while I am giving myself to you," he pumps with such gentleness. Damn, no man has ever said that shit to me before. It turns me on even more. I roll over and climb on top of his muscular body and climb up on his erect dick and straddle him, riding him slow and sensually, which arouses him to stick his finger in his mouth and saturate it with his spit. He then massages my hard nipples with it. The sensation arouses me as he gently flips me on my back and licks my protruding clit. My hips rotate, as the swishing sound of pussy juice turns us both on. I pant, "Yes, yes, yessssssss muthafucker! You want it, don't you! Don't you?" He moans, "Yesssss, yessss!" He sticks three of his fingers in my anal which sparks a charge of adrenaline that shoots down to my clit. My body quivers. Damn! Being pleasured is an understatement. Xavier is fucking me like he is trying to win my love.

"Ahhhh! Baby, don't stop…!" I demand with my eyes rolling in the back of my head. Smack! Smack! "Ooh, baby, smack that ass again." I say, moaning, biting down on my bottom lip.

Oh, the sensation triggers this electricity that zooms throughout my whole body. I am so fuckin' hot. The thrill makes me nearly bump my head on the headboard because it feels so fuccccccckin' good!

"Both of you turn over," Xavier softly says in shallow breaths. His body of vitality leads me to believe that he can go for hours and hours.

My hands grip the headboard; ass is mid-air, and so does Eerie, while he is in between my legs pumping his cock in me doggy-style. I wail and wince for mercy, "Fuck me, shit! Ah, ah, ah! Ooh! Ooh! Ooh, baby! Shit! Shit! Shiiiittttt!" I bite down on my bottom lip with sweat dripping down my face. Ooooooh, he is giving me the dick just the way I like it…hard. He is f-u-c-k-ing the shit out of me.

He slouches his face down and licks the crack of my ass and slips his middle finger in my pussy hole again and finger-fucks me. I nearly choke on my spit especially when he rubs my big tits with his hot hands and pulls on my clit making my body shudder into earth-shattering orgasms. "FUCK, FUCK, FUCK!!!" I scream biting my upper lip. Then Xavier pleasures Eerie in the same manner. We switch positions with him reclined on the bed. My fingers tightly clench the headboard as I ride him with my titties flopping against my supple skin, trying to rub his dick raw. Suddenly there is a downpour of rain drizzling out of me. I squint, as the feel is so intense. All I want to do is keep fucking, to pleasure my starved body. I can't compose my pussy…"Eat-'Em-Up." I guess her trifling ass needs to fuck just as much as I do.

We fuck for 45 minutes. Then Xavier rolls me over and slowly eats me out again. I kick and moan and squint and scream by the feel of his long sodden tongue upon my flesh. OMG! By the time he is through he is foaming at the mouth. Shit, I feel back in mint condition. I don't have a care in the fuckin' world. Nada one. Okay, maybe one… *Christopher*. Eerie is sucking on his toes as she slithers up and begins to lick the head of his dick and then slithers further down to lick and suck on his peanut-colored balls.

Well, once we take a breather, Xavier starts jerking his dick until it gets hard again. All I do is smile because he makes me feel so fuckin' sexy. Something Christopher has forgotten how to do. I can't believe Avery had all of this, this lusciousness and didn't know what to do with it. A woman knows when a man's needs haven't been met. He practically ravished my body. I smile from ear to ear because

Avery just allowed me to open her unopened door. And I am going to do whatever it takes to push her out of his mind and then his heart. No, I don't have to love him, to fuck him. All I have to do is be at his every beck and call. Sooner or later he'll forget about her and I'll become his main squeeze, of course, with Eerie as our sidekick. What man wouldn't want his woman to bring home free pussy?

Stacy

Listen. I had a big, big fetish: women, strippers, and homemaker hookers. I guess you can call Nymph a sex fiend. She didn't stand a chance messing wit' me. I was wayyyyy out of her league. But she'd begged to differ. She let my looks, my status of being a founder for a nonprofit cloud her judgment. So what I stole my boy Xavier's identity! Fuck him! 'Ey, that muthafucka ain't worth shit in my book anyway. Uh-huh. The cocky muthafuka slept wit' my girl. Look, I don't give a damn if it was last week or last year, the fact of the matter is, we were 'sposed to be boys. There is a code of conduct between men and Xavier broke the code so what am I to do, shitttt, do the same muthafuckin' thing. No, I don't care about two wrongs don't make a right. He was wrong for what he did now I'm about to make it right. Like I said, fuck him! You wait and see.

Anyway, Nymph wanted out of the 'hood and figured dealing with a man with money would be her ticket out of the projects (Langston-Lynch). Wrong!!!!!

First, I was a nobody. And secondly, I didn't have money. I hooked up wit' her just to get her welfare check even knowing that she had four mouths to feed. Fuck those kids! I didn't care about them. They weren't my kids. Hell, I didn't even claim the kids I had. I had that bitch dangling from a string. I told her my name was Johnson Perry. And she believed every word I spoke.

Johnson reeled her in quite nicely. He promised her so many things, and delivered on those promises, except one. He didn't know how to be faithful. You got it. He was a nigga bitch too.

Johnson was a cocky nigga bitch—an arrogant ass muthafucker. He thought the world revolved around him. You couldn't tell him that his shit didn't stink. He'd tell you you were wrong. Someone had to knock some sense back into his head. But no one did, not even Nymph. She merely accepted him and all that came with him…drama. Why? She was desperate and tired, dreaming of a better tomorrow. Hell, being a welfare mom she wanted out with the old and in with the new—a new man with some new money and some new dick. She wanted a man to set her up nicely where she could continue to sit on her big ass and do nothing but watch cable and stuff her face. The days were long and hard for her and her four nappy-headed kids. But that didn't push her to get up off of her ass and try to find a job. She depended on the system. The system spoiled her. She had no ambition, no motivation. All she had was looks, long hair, and a functional pussy. She worked the hell out of that pussy too. She didn't want to fall victim to a hustler-type of dude again because she knew eventually he'd be locked up like all of her four baby daddies. She wanted a successful man. One that could bail his own ass out if he'd gotten locked up. One that could provide the necessities that she felt she and her nappy-headed kids deserved. The one problem Nymph had was that she never wanted to pull her own weight. She became deadweight and Johnson said, fucks that!

Nymph was fine, don't get me wrong, but she was an uneducated woman. I mean being in her mid-thirties you'd think she had some common sense. Not Nymph. She stood about 5'8" coated in mocha skin with auburn mane and the prettiest teeth. Damn, she had some pretty teeth! Nymph was dense, though. Nymph ain't know shit but how to give good head and how to hold her hand out. She was what I called a "Gimme Bitch." She ain't have no skill and didn't want to learn one either. She ain't know how to cook. She kept her house dirty. She ain't know how to do laundry or braid her daughters hair. Her sons looked like nappy-headed orphans. She had no grace about her. She was merely a fuck. Johnson no longer wanted her, her pussy, her ass, or to hear her mouthpiece. And he definitely didn't want her four nappy-headed kids. To him, she was black trash waiting for a handout. And he wasn't going to give it to her. So he dropped her. And she was furious. She turned into one of those fatal attraction chicks. Nymph lost her grip. And Johnson played that bitch out.

Johnson was in search of a woman with some clout and some long paper. His main squeeze would be a woman with class and style and sex appeal. Nymph tried to mimic, but underneath it all it just wasn't her. She was too fuckin' ghetto. Cussing and fussing like a ghetto chick when she couldn't have her way. She was still a baby in Johnson's eyes. At least she acted that way. And Johnson didn't have the patience to mold a grimy rat into rich bitch. Nymph was a project rat. And for some reason, Nymph had a problem accepting it. She wouldn't let go. And it only made matters worse for her.

With all this pussy out here Johnson had no concerns. He had money. Nymph's money. Money could buy pussy. Since Nymph wanted him so bad, she'd let Johnson pimp her out just to be close to him. And that nigga bitch did. He figured he'd make a profit off of her pretty ghetto ass. And he did. The nigga bitches were pouncing dat ass, too. They were paying him fifty dollars a fuck. Nymph only got ten percent of that. And she thought she was getting paid. That dumb bitch! Lol.

Nymph made a name for herself, but she didn't care, because now she was getting paid for her efforts and still collecting her welfare check. The only problem was her kids suffered. At least before she met Johnson, her kids had a mother, food, clothes, and a roof over their heads. But after Johnson hooked her up with her new gig, shit, her kids got lost in the system. DYFS took her kids away. Nymph had long abandoned them as well as herself. 'Ey, that was not Johnson's problem. Fuck her, he'd quickly say and bounce.

Avery

I come to.

My mouth tastes pasty like cotton balls are stuck to the roof of it. The life as I knew it has changed without my knowledge as if my existence was stripped from my body. I can't believe this is happening to me. That Stacy would stoop so low as to satisfy himself. But if I sit and think about it I shouldn't be too surprised.

"What did you do?" I ask as Stacy is sitting on the heather-blue leather sectional across from me reading the newspaper.

"What do you mean, what did I do?" he licked his index finger and turned the page.

"You know. Don't play with me, Sta-."

He chuckles, and then narrow-eyes me. "Who do you think you're talkin' to, bitch?"

I ignore the word *bitch*. "Stacy, just tell me."

"Look. I'm givin' you paradise. You don't like it?"

My eyes scroll around the spaciously modern furnished home. "Where am I?"

"Home."

"This is not my home." I happen to look down and on my ring finger is a sparkling 5-carat oval diamond ring. This ring musta cost him a fortune. Something I'm beginning to realize Stacy does not have. I can't believe this man is holding me hostage possibly in someone else's house. I can't believe he has abducted me like some crazed predator.

"Where am I?" I ask again, still looking around the living room.

He leans forward in his black and silver silk pajamas and says, "I told you. You're home. This is our home."

I shake my head no. "This is not my home, my apartment. Where am I? Tell me where I am?" By now I am hysterical.

Stacy rises to his feet and comes and sits next to me on the sectional. He takes his hands and places mine in the middle like a peanut butter and jelly sandwich and says in a mellow tone, "Avery, we are home."

"What do you mean 'we'?"

Immediately I feel this sick feeling in my gut.

"We" as in us, our, home," he says with a grimace.

I shake my head again, bewildered. "No, no, this doesn't make sense to me."

"What?"

"This. Us. We..."

"What are you sayin' woman...th-th-that you regret us getting married! Me providing you with all of this...this fine shit! What you don't want it? You want something else. What do you want, Avery, huh? Tell me what the fuck you want and I'll get it for you, baby," he says while looking at me with this dirty look in his eyes.

I blink triple times. "MARRIED! Did you just say MARRIED! WHAT DO YOU MEAN MARRIED! I NEVER GOT MARRIED TO YOU...WHY WOULD I MARRY YOU YOU DON'T LOVE ME AND I DON'T LOVE YOU!" I suck back in some air and try to catch my breath with a glare in my bloodshot red eyes. What did he do...drug me with a Forget Pill. I know he did something, something to make me forget and pass out for days at a time.

Stacy lowers his voice. "Av, baby, I asked you to marry me and you said yes. We had a few of our friends there."

My forehead crumples. "WAIT! FRIENDS?! I don't have any friends! Enemies, yes! Friends, no!"

"Woman, calm da fuck down!" Stacy says with a mean look in his eyes.

I squint my eyes at him, "What have you done? You don't love me. And I don't love you."

Stacy shouts at the top of his lungs, "Yes, I do!"

I sway my head from side to side, in disbelief.

"And you do love me. You told me so. You told me before God, bitch."

"No, no, no!" I snap with eyes overflowing with tears.

Stacy smirks. "What are you going to do about it anyway? We've been married for two weeks now."

"TWO WEEKS!" I snap again. At this point I cannot compose myself. The same reaction I had when Dr. Fulmore told me that I am HIV-positive, I have again, but this time I react with full force. I land on top of his body and start punching him with iron fists in his face. *Wham! Wham! Wham!* Then I scream, "You stupid muthafucker! How could you do this to me!"

Stacy wraps his arms around my waist and tussles with me to the floor and starts wailing on me like some dude on the streets. Blood runs from my nose. My left eye swells the size of a tennis ball, but I keep trying to fight him back. Tears stream down my face, full force.

At the time I am not worried about him kicking my ass. I've

taken a beaten from him before. Numerous times. And then want to come around me and kiss and makeup like I'm gonna suddenly develop amnesia and forget all the shit he has put me through. That ain't never gonna happen. I'll always remember. Always.

"Oh, you'a tough one, huh?" Stacy pulls me by the arm and spins me on my butt as he drags me across the hardwood floor and opens the door to this closet and locks me in.

"Let me out, Stacy! Let me out!" I bang my fists against the hardwood door with tears rushing down my face. My body is quivering. The only thing I can concentrate on is that Stacy drugged me up and coerced this marriage. But why would he go through such lengths to marry a woman he does not know or love? Why manipulate me into something that I never wanted. Is he trying to drive me insane?

For three agonizing days I sit in the closet with no food, water, or even the decency to take a shower. I bang on the door again. "Why are you doing this to me? You don't love me. You don't even know me. You know nothing about me. My family. My upbringing. My struggles. Whether I'm in good health or not…" I raise a brow. Wait a minute, I think to myself. If we got married as he says we did, wouldn't we have to have taken a blood test? And if that were the case he would've found out that I am HIV-positive, right?

I hear footsteps walking toward the door; I wonder if it's Stacy. The door unlocks. I turn the knob and step out. Face-to-face I stand before him. "Pew! You stink!" Stacy waves his hand with a scrunch up nose. Don't, I know it. He has something behind his back. What is it? I don't know. He brings his left arm forward and shows me what looks like a certificate of some sort. If I didn't see it with my very own eyes I would've never believed it. He places in my hands a marriage certificate. Why? I wonder.

Who would have known? I did not see him for who he truly was in the very beginning. Or maybe I chose not to. Who is this imposture that now stands before me with his fists balled, bitter with rage in his eyes? Where is the man that I was forcefully made to fall hopelessly in love with? The man I married for worse, not better? What have I done to deserve a life like this? How could I have missed the signs?

I don't love him. It's been nearly four months and Stacy constantly reminds me of how much he loves me by punching and kicking me, and leaving ugly bruises on my body. I continuously make up excuses for his actions. I make sure I prepare myself for when he walks through the front door. His dinner is hot and already set on the kitchen table. I make sure his clothes are clean, pressed, and folded. I pick up the debris alongside the house, mow the lawn, and take out the trash so everything is in order and he'll be happy with me. I thought things were going to change and we were going to live a blissful life of togetherness. How foolish I was to think that. I wonder if it was possible that he misunderstood what "vows" meant. I can tell you what they don't mean to me.

He did not take a "vow" to use me as his punching bag and then bring me home flowers with an apology. The "vow" did not include keeping me locked up in this house. Stacy has used our marriage to falsely make accusations to give him a reason to go out and "play." Then on top of that, he not only listens to my telephone conversations, but also has the audacity to tap our phone. To make matters even worse, he takes what he wants from between my legs, forcefully, and then says that I gave an "unsatisfactory" performance.

I deserve better. He reminds me of … God; I am so damn tired of wasting my life away with a man who does not appreciate me.

Yeah, how many times, ladies', have you heard or even said that same thing? We often say it over and over in our minds, but, we continue to sit our dumb asses in the same pool drenched with our own blood. When is it going to stop?

I pretend that one day my husband will walk through the front door and be a totally different man. I pray day and night for my daydream to come true. Unfortunately, it doesn't. The situation worsens and my abuse becomes more visible. I try using makeup to cover the blackened eyes and bruised cheeks, but the pain is written on my face.

I scream in silence. I won't pick up the phone at home because I know Stacy has it tapped. Sure, I can easily call from my cellular, but he's followed me before, and who's to say that he still won't come after me if I leave him. In fact, he has threatened to kill me if I ever look like I am leaving him. It seems so easy for someone who is not living the life to say, "She's stupid." But I am living the life and my life is something I want to continue to live. Fear keeps me on a leash like a dog. I'm afraid of the outcome. Understand my point of view; listen to what I'm saying.

I keep seeing these images in my head where I am being stabbed numerous times—thirty-two times, to be exact. And Stacy still is not satisfied. I've visualized blood pumping out of my body like it's flowing from a water fountain, but Stacy is there, lunging the knife into me again and again, as if I am not human, like he's out of control, as if I don't matter. He continues to stab me over and over and over again. I can't even begin to tell you how distressed I feel at these times. I shake my head to make sure it is a vision, and not reality.

I keep seeing the man I do not love choking me to death. My face is purple; eyes are bulging as he tries to strangle the life out of me. I'm gasping for air; he looks at me with those blue eyes and spits in my face like I'm his "nigger bitch."

Ladies', I feel like I should be going to Leap of Faith Funeral Home to make pre-arrangements, type-set my obituary to read:

Avery Love, 45, born and raised in Paterson, New Jersey, she was the only daughter of her predeceased parents Cashmere Withering-Love and Poppa Love. She was a member of Temple Cross Baptist Church in Paterson, for many years. Avery was a former entrepreneur of a performance arts gallery called Anonymous. Previous to that she was a paralegal for Bruman & Prescott Law firm in lower Manhattan for several years. She leaves behind, her deceitful spouse, Stacy Blazman. Good riddance.

I see a reason for leaving. Leaving before this premature obituary becomes my reality. Everyday I'm afraid. But I know that love is not supposed to hurt. Love should not leave an imprint on my skin. Love should not mess-up my mind so that my self-esteem diminishes. It should not make me feel like a dog instead of a human being. I am a woman! Unfortunately, his wife! And that does not give him a reason to control me, or beat me senselessly. I refuse to live in darkness any longer. I refuse!

With tears rolling down my face, body trembling, I find the strength within me to leave Stacy, as I found the strength to leave others in my past. I look at the telephone, knowing that it is tapped, and pray for the extra strength to ask for help. I work up the courage when someone answers the hotline and they connect me to a shelter for battered women. I take a deep breath and I do as I am instructed, as I rehearsed, quickly. Ms. Danetta tells me to hurry and pack any important belongings, and not to call anyone else because even an acquaintance might let Stacy know what I am doing. She tells me to pull myself together, to calm myself down. She can hear the fear in my heart. I am scared out of my mind.

"Avery, Avery, calm down." Ms. Danetta says, and then tells me to leave the house immediately, and to go Mahogany Women's

Shelter and to ask for Jodie Steely. But I don't, for some unknown reason. I do stuff my Nicole Miller satchel while watching the front door. I am a nervous wreck, afraid that my husband will come walking through it and catch me leaving him. Lord knows I am afraid that if he does, I will be dead. My obituary will become a reality. I realize at this moment how soaked my favorite lime-green T-shirt has become. My body is perspiring profusely. My eyes track every noise. I resume my nail biting, a habit I'd abandoned when I moved into my own apartment, but re-established after dating Stacy. I notice bloodied cuticles and fingertips on both hands. My feet cannot walk out the front door, for whatever reason. My mind is paralyzed, with the rest of my body. I cannot move even if I have to. I say a silent prayer asking the Lord to take me to Mahogany Women's Shelter, which enables me to finally walk out the door and down the street to the bodega on the corner. I use my cell phone inside to call a taxi. Then I wait outside.

I am paranoid. I keep looking over my shoulder and then at my watch. I flinch whenever a car horn honks. I think I am going to lose it right here in front of the store, but I don't. The taxi arrives and I quickly get in. I keep praying all the way to the shelter. As I exit the taxi the Lord stays with me, walking me into the shelter. When I give the receptionist, a slender, white, mousy-haired woman, with sapphire blue eyes my name, she tells me to follow her into a little room off the waiting area. There are fifteen women inside, attending a group meeting, who all share my pain. I never realized how many other women were living my nightmare. They have all survived as battered women, victims of domestic violence. I no longer feel alone. If anything, I have learned to be alone and live my life.

The next day, I keep hearing the serenity prayer in my head: *God grant me the Serenity to accept the things I cannot change… the Courage to change the things I can…and the Wisdom to know the difference.* It makes me take a stand and step. I enter the doors of Thin Line Rehabilitation Center and tell the black sister who is sitting at the desk dressed in a black T-shirt with hot pink lettering that reads: The Write Message, with thick twists of dark brown hair that I am an addict. That's exactly what I say: *addict.* Hopefully it is the beginning to my end of self-inflicted pain.

***

I receive a call a few weeks ago from a woman named Hippa

Thatcher, who is a writer for a women's magazine called RAINBIRDS. Hippa asks if I'd be interested in telling the story of my life, with all the leaps and bounds that catapulted me into the world spotlight. At first, I am hesitant, fearing the return of a life filled with unrelenting pain, the rape, HIV, the emotional and physical abuse, the abusive, harmful names that I have left behind. I realize I am blessed to be able to tell my story. Some people don't have this privilege. And that is what I consider this opportunity to be, a privilege. If I am willing to share with others, I might find a way to heal myself, too.

Hippa arrives at Thin Line Rehabilitation Center promptly at 1:00 p.m. She signs in with her photographer, a tall, lanky, unattractive man with bisque skin, hazel eyes and a bushy Afro, sets up in the cafeteria. There is no comparison to the life I have grown accustomed to, and my being in front of the camera in this facility with Hippa, the short ivory-complexion woman with bright strawberry hair, freckles on her nose and cheeks, vibrant sapphire-blue eyes and a body that can stop an eighteen-wheeler truck in one hundred miles per hour speed. Hippa has the most infectious English accent I have ever heard. I can literally listen to her talk for hours upon hours. My life is different now; no more glamour and glitz, those days are forever over for me.

Hippa and I speak candidly while the photographer prepares to take shots. She expresses her appreciation for me wanting to share my life with other models or people in general who are or once were drug addicts. Our interview continues below:

HIPPA: *Avery, when did things begin to change in your life?*

AVERY: *Honestly, the rape, then HIV, then being shot, and then becoming a model. I could not believe that I was chosen to be a model. My life was moving so fast I became overwhelmed. I wanted the spotlight so badly that I needed something to lift my spirits. I met a man at one of the photo shoots who introduced me to cocaine. Cocaine became my best friend and I seemed to be flying high on life. I had spunk and energy. I felt myself rising to the top and then slowly I slid back down the pole into a well of despair. I was snorting coke on the regular and my funds got low. I started missing photo shoots, being late most of the time when I did show up, and my body was getting thinner by the day.*

HIPPA: *When you talk about cocaine it seems as if it was your companion. Was that how you perceived it to be?*

AVERY: Cocaine would soothe all of my pain away, no matter what was wrong. I felt powerful and in control like nothing could hurt me ever again. Yes, I believed it was my companion. That was my past.

HIPPA: Do you believe the spotlight changed your perception of yourself?

AVERY: Growing up I was invisible, except to be ridiculed. As a model I was attractive. It reminded me of how I used to feel about myself, back at a time when my life seemed golden. People who never would have noticed me admired me in front of the camera. I was told that I was going places. Word of advice: Never believe everything that is told to you. I can't blame anyone, but myself for the life that I live presently.

HIPPA: Do you have any idea of a career goal if you don't continue modeling?

AVERY: My career came so quickly and with a blink of an eye it was gone. I have no sense of direction as to which path I'll take, but I know that I need to continue to commit to this rehab. This is my career goal, to remain clean.

HIPPA: Do you see any strides from when you first walked through those doors?

AVERY: I was at my lowest when I entered those doors and God helps lift me up. It had to take me sleeping in an alley somewhere, naked, when the police took me to the hospital. Apparently I had sex or was raped, I didn't even remember, which. Couldn't even tell you with whom. I had been robbed and beaten. I guess you can say that was the guiding light that brought me here, to try to save what was left of me. No one came to my rescue, no one was concerned about my whereabouts, and no one reported me missing because they knew I was a junky. Avery is a junky! That's all they knew. You gave me a chance to redeem all that by letting me help others with my story. Yes, I see strides because I am no longer living in denial.

HIPPA: Are you involved with anyone at this present time? Do you have family and friends for support?

AVERY: Presently, I am alone, not lonely, but content. I used to be uncomfortable with who I was before I became a model. I was very lonely as a child and as a young adult. Cocaine stayed with me like nobody else had, used to be my steady companion. It made passionate love to my mind and body. I did things that were other than acceptable, just to feed my habit, back then. But cocaine is no longer my mate.

HIPPA: *Do you feel any shame for being a drug addict?*

AVERY: *Am I ashamed? Not at all. I am in my glory because I am still here and I face my demons every day. This is just another learning experience for me to share.*

HIPPA: *What do you see for your future?*

AVERY: *Hmmm? There are so many things, but the main one is to commit to a lifestyle that is non-destructive. My modeling career is over and to be perfectly honest with you, I don't want it back. I have a fresh start and a chance to put my best foot forward. Often times your destiny is not too far behind you. It could be staring you in the face without your knowledge.*

HIPPA: *What is presently staring you in your face?*

AVERY: *Life....*

Stacy

"DeNetria! Yo' DeNetria! Wassup girl? What you doing in Paterson?" I say getting an eyeful of her. Damn she looks good. I wonder if she'll let me eat her pussy.

DeNetria shakes her head from side to side. "Nothing. What brings you back to your neck-of-the-woods?" she asks in a salty tone.

I had taken a trip to Virginia to spend some quality time with this white bitch I met on Tagged. Actually, I was on the run again after I got word that that bitch husband was hot on my trail.

"Figured I'd come back. What 'bout you?"

"Just doing me. Taking care of *our* kids. I have some unfinished business I have to take care of..."

"'Ey do you." I say nonchalantly.

DeNetria's forehead crumples. "You ain't gonna ask about your kids." She twists her lips in disgust and folds her arms about her chest.

I shake my head from side to side. "You just gotta start, don't you? Can't never be..." I wave my hand in her face. "Forget it. I'm out." I step off.

She yells. "Just to let you know, your kids are in the dark!"

I stop and turn around because she is putting her business out in the streets. I walk back over to her. I have a grimace on my face and I narrow-eye her. "Bitch, what did you just say?"

DeNetria places her hands on her small waist. "I said your kids are in the dark. I ran into some financial problems and I couldn't afford to pay the light bill. I figured food in our kids' mouths was more important, you know. I just need a little help before DYFS gets involved. Um, since you are their father I figured who better to ask."

My eyes droop and darken. "Aren't you getting child support from me?"

"Yeah. I had to use that for other expenses. I have a lot on my plate, STACY!"

I stand tall and emotionless. "Well, you're asking the wrong nigga."

DeNetria stands still not surprised, but pissed, as usual. Her eyes are watery, but she doesn't shed a tear. She knows better than to get her hopes up high thinking that I will come around and want to

118

be a father to our kids. She can keep on wondering, hoping, wishing that I'd think about what I was doing to them, to her. When is he going to get it, huh? I swear I can hear her thinking. When? I keep hearing her ask herself that same question. Unfortunately I don't think she'll ever receive an answer to that question 'cause I don't give a fuck! I think heartlessly as I swagger off down the street. Fuck her and them black ass kids of hers, I mumble underneath my breath making my way down lower Main Street.

It is April Fool's Day, and I guess DeNetria feels like the biggest fool of them all. I ain't have an ounce of remorse in my bloodstream about how I feel for those kids. Her kids. Whatever! DeNetria keeps trying to push those kids off on me. I told her a thousand times. I warned her on more than one occasion. I didn't want to hear it anymore.

It may sound insensitive. So what! I don't care. I even threatened her, but obviously she didn't take me seriously. I bet she does now, I say to myself.

As I am walking down lower Main Street about to turn in Record City to hollah at my nigga Hunt I bump into my two childhood niggas: Victor Stash and Lou Bassett.

"Yo niggas, whassup?" I throw my arms mid-air with a huge smile on my face.

Victor and Lou give me a brotherly hug.

"Long time no see, man." Victor says delightfully. Boy he sure looks different. He is tall, every bit of six feet five inches, brown-skinned with wire-framed glasses on looking like a professor with his tan Dickey's and plait short sleeved shirt on. What I found pretty funny is that he talked educated. You know proper like the white folks he'd been hanging around. He says he is an engineer for Google. I always knew he was the brainy act of our crew. He says he also volunteers as a Big Brother for troubled teens. Good for him, I think to myself. 'Cause I could care less about these thugs out here— don't fuck wit' me and I won't fuck wit' you, is basically how I feel.

It really hit me when Victor tells me that his mother had passed away. Damn. Mrs. Stash was a beautiful woman—a kindhearted and gentle soul.

"Yeah, man, mom's is gone. She had breast cancer."

"Ah man, sorry to hear that." I sincerely say. "You a'ight?"

Victor belly laughs, "Yeah, man. I mean it took me some years to get used to her not being here. Not hearing her voice, hearing her contagious laugh, seeing her smile so wide when I got my degrees. I have moments to cherish with mom—fond memories. That means a lot these days. Death is something, you know."

Lou and I both nod our heads simultaneously.

It seems the sensitive side of me will show when it comes to my male friends, but for these bitches, forget it. I'd hardened up in a heartbeat. I don't feel the need to show them my sensitive side probably because they'd take it for granted. Nah. That ain't gonna happen to me again. Never again!

Lou Bassett works for Greyhound in Atlanta. He is a mechanic. That doesn't surprise me because as kids he was always helping his step dad work on his Oldsmobile.

"Yeah man, I own a soul food restaurant too, called MY LEFTOVERS." Lou says enthusiastically.

I laugh when he tells me this. It just sounded country as hell to me. Nothing really changed as far as how he looks. I mean face wise he still looks like the kid, but older. He stands about six feet two. He has a potbelly. His dark-skinned face is clean-shaven and his head is bald. He wears glasses too. He has on a pair of brown khakis and a light-blue polo shirt and a pair of tan loafers on his size fourteen feet.

"Yo whatever happened to Thomas and Bryant?" I ask crossing my arms about my chest.

Lou shakes his head and deeply sighs, and then he speaks in his baritone voice. "Well, I heard through the grapevine that Thomas got caught up in the drug game in Baltimore. I heard he got killed about four years ago."

"Damn." I reply. I don't know what to say.

Victor interjects in his mellow tone. "As far as Bryant, well, I heard he lives in Pasadena, California, with his wife and five children. He owns a couple of franchises. Bryant is a millionaire. I haven't heard from him lately, though. I think the last time we spoke was when he was visiting in New York. He's still easygoing. The money didn't go to his head."

"Nah," I say, wide-eyed.

Victor and Lou both sway their heads from side to side.

"Nope. Bryant is pretty down-to-earth." Lou confirms. "So what's up with you, dude?" Lou asks as he adjusts his glasses on his round face.

I feel like I am under the microscope. Damn.

"Well, I got my bachelor's in Accounting." I suck my teeth. "But unfortunately, I haven't done much with it lately. Got caught up in some other shit and got sidetracked."

They both give me their undivided attention. Lou scratches his throat and then says, "Well, dude, only you can get back on the horse. We figured you would be the first to get out of Paterson as much as you used to talk about leaving this place. Find your way back and do what you were destined to do."

I massage my chin. "That's the problem. I'm not sure what my purpose is anymore."

Victor looks me dead in my eyes as if he sees something. He talks with his hands that look like two lethal weapons. "You know where to go for the answer if you really want to know. There is always one man listening. All you have to do is talk and ask for guidance. He'll guide you in the right direction when you're ready."

On that note, I remain silent.

"We must do dinner while we're still in town," Victor says. "How's your schedule looking for tomorrow evening?"

"Open." I reply, followed by a chuckle. "Listen; give me your numbers so that we can keep in touch."

We exchange numbers in our cell phones, give each other another brotherly hug, and part ways.

I stop in Record City to say whassup to Hunt. He stands about 6 feet tall, light-skinned with a big ass gap in-between his two front teeth. He's a wacky kind of nigga, a practical joker. He's the type that keeps your spirits up. As long as I've known him, he doesn't let too much get to him. He takes life in stride. He'll tell you to go fuck yourself in a minute, if you rub him the wrong way. He's crazy like that. Haven't met too many brothers like him. Yeah. He's cool people.

Hunt and I parlay for a bit.

"How's your brother Joey doing?" I ask him.

"Oh, he's hanging in there, doing dialysis." Hunt says.

"Next time you see or talk to him tell him I said wassup."

"All right, boss." Hunt salutes me like he is in the service. I just crack a smile.

"Man, you are still goofy as ever." I say as I bob my head to Mary J. Blige's "HOOD LOVE."

Hunt plays some oldies but goodies and then I head home to change out of my thug wear and head over to Nymph's crib to see what the crazy bitch is up to. Actually, I go to pickup my money and since my balls are aching, figured I get some pussy to go. There is no way Nymph will tell Johnson no. The bitch is a fiend. I mean she needs dick like I need air to breathe.

I enter Langston-Lynch projects dressed in my True Religion jeans and white V-neck T-shirt with my low profile black leather slip-on Jack Purcell converse on. Dolce & Gabbana "the one" cascades in the lobby as I press the elevator button to the 6th floor. It takes every bit of ten minutes for the elevator to come. I hop on and exit off. Walk down the hall, stop in front of 6T, insert my key in Nymph's door, and walk in.

I startle Nymph and her guest as they are indulging in each other. To my utter surprise, it is Asbury.

"Asbury, what the fucks are you doing here?" I say with a crumpled forehead. I have to do something before my cover is blown. I had no idea that Asbury is bisexual. Damn, nigga you slipping, I say to myself.

Asbury doesn't know what to say. Obviously I caught her with her pants down, lime green panties down to her ankles, and her legs cocked open with Nymph's face in between her thighs. They are on the floor lying on top of a sheet and Asbury's head is resting on one of the four oversized multicolored throw pillows.

"Johnson, what's going on?" Nymph asks.

Asbury purses her lips. "Yeah, Johnson! Who da fuck is Johnson, huh, Stacy?"

This bitch put me on blast. I am cold busted so the only thing I can do is play this shit up and out.

Nymph cuts her eyes from side to side. "You two know each other?"

I remain calm. Put on some Blair Underwood flavor. I snicker. "Listen, you bitches don't get to ask me questions. I ask the muthafucking questions." I grab my dick, palm and squeeze it as their mouths water. "This muthafucker asks the questions. Now where the fuck is my money, bitch?!"

Nymph hops up and heads toward her bedroom. I follow as I lust for her perfectly shaped ass. Shit, I am already rock hard by the time I enter her bedroom. I push her naked body on the bed and stick my dick in her wet, wet, wet pussy. Damn, her pussy feels like spit is oozing out of it. It is slippery like a slope.

A few minutes later, Asbury enters the room in her birthday suit. I guess she feels left out. Her body is glistening. I have two bitches in Nymph's bed.

Nymph's ass is in my face as I lick her pussy while she is sucking my joint. Asbury is squeezing Nymph's melon sized titties and sucking her nipples. Those babies are rock hard. We all switch positions with Asbury kneeling on her knees. I am giving it to her doggy-style while Nymph is getting her pussy eaten out by Asbury. I am pouncing Asbury's round ass.

Nymph's fingers grips the cast iron headboard as Asbury is

slurping her juices. She rests her feet on Asbury's sheer back. All of us are moaning. Sweat is dripping down my face. My dick is getting harder and harder. I yank on Asbury's hair weave and pull out a track. She doesn't feel a thing. My dick is throbbing.

"Damn! Shit! Shit! Fuck!" I spew out in one breath.

My dick wants to explode. I am about to bust a nutt in this bitch. I pull out and stick my dick in Asbury's ass and fuck the shit outta her. I fuck her so fuckin' hard I have this bitch screaming Nymph's name. Lol. That shit turns me on so much that I bust another nutt in her ass with my big ass dick. Shitttttt, come splatters all over her inner walls. Talk about fireworks. It is more likes cherry bombs. Shit, I give that bitch a come bath. Then I tell her to get the fuck out while I get my second nut by fuckin' the shit outta Nymph. Damn. Her pussy is creamy moist.

As soon as I start licking her pussy my dick is rock hard again. I stick it in and hit the pit of her pussy. I have her climbing the fuckin' walls. Then I bust a nut and splatter come all over her titties and face. The bitch loves it. I feel like the king that I am. Huh, I killed two bitches with one dick. Can't nobody tell me that I ain't the man. Nobody. The whole scene could've been a catastrophe but I managed to think on my feet. That's how a nigga show and proves. It's not always what he says or how he says it. Nah. It's more in his performance that keeps his bitches in check.

I jump in the shower to get those bitches smell off of me. Towel dry and glide some Gillette Odor Shield under my armpits. I exit the bathroom, head back into the bedroom and throw my clothes back on, and then grab my cash off the black lacquer dresser. I leave Nymph sound asleep on her bed butt naked wit' a smile on her face. The bitch just ought to be cheesing after I done gave her this muthafuckin' dick.

I walk into the living room to find Asbury sitting on the black couch engrossed in a movie. At first, I don't pay much attention until I see two muthafuckers kissing.

"What the fuck you watching?" I ask Asbury.

She ignores me.

"Why you watching that 'faggot' shit?" I ask her again.

For some unknown reason I find myself intrigued as if this force is pulling me in. As bad as I want to walk out the door I can't. Something is forcefully making me stand there like my kicks are cemented to the floor. I slowly walk over to the couch, sit down, and watch the movie. I don't move a muscle. I don't blink an eye. My eyes are glued to the screen watching some HBO documentary about living on the down low. I remembered hearing about this movie from this dude named Jump in the streets. Yeah, Jump is a movie junkie. But then I nix that shit off 'cause I ain't bent over gettin' fucked in the ass. For some strange reason I find myself caught up in the moment as if I am looking at a reflection of myself. Then my mind drifts back to Rubin "Hurricane" Carter—a black man fighting for more. No, I was never a prizefighter, but I feel like I am fighting in the ring of the jungle (ghetto) every day. Fighting to get out of the gutter. But for some reason I ain't giving my best jabs, uppercuts or left hooks like Rubin. Nah. I am bullshitting myself. Playing my own self out like a fuckin' nigga bitch.

"Nigga, what you want!" Wino's voice snaps back in my head and it annoys me.

What this muthafucker want now? I ask myself. I see that drunken muthafucker hunched over sitting on that stoop in front Gene's Liquors. I ignore his voice and continue on that nowhere path of self-destruction. Until it finally hits me—

It hits me hard in my gut like someone has knocked the shit outta me. I see Wino up on his feet swinging. He sneaks a nigga with another fast jab to my gut and I begin to spit up blood. What does this all mean, I ask myself?

Slowly I'd come to the realization that I am just another nigga in the 'hood trying to make a dollar with no common sense, drive, or the ability to see my way out. What is holding a nigga down? The answer to that significant question I still don't know. I feel another hot blow to my gut. *"You know… you sorry ass muthafucker!"* I hear Wino say. Then that drunken muthafucker sneaks a nigga again with a sucker punch. Ouch! I grit down on my teeth. My temples pop out and eyes darken and droop. I hate another black man calling me a *"nigga bitch"*! Oooooo-kay, okay, I can deal with the "I-ain't-shit" part because there is some truth to that, but to be called out your name messes wit' a nigga's head. I got sidetracked most of my life. Feeling as though I always had to work extra hard to prove my capabilities. I always had to push myself. Pump myself up to believe that I could do anything any other nigga could do and be successful, but that one word "nigga" broke the black man I used to be. It broke me down to a little man. It broke me down to nothing—to think that I was worth nothin'. I became a *"nigga bitch"* and it changed me for the worse, not the better. I became a beast in my own body. The word took over my mind and changed my thinking about the freedom I once possessed. I willingly handed over possession of my soul to the inner demon and changed into this person I never perceived myself to be. I was a black educated man in my prime. But as a nine-year-old boy the seed had already been planted in my brain: *"Nigga, you ain't shit!"* How could one word influence the possibilities of my existence? Easily. I gave it power. And the power overruled the man. And the man became a replica of his unknown father—a deadbeat—a no good nigga bitch!

Avery

Home sweet home, I say to myself. Time sure has flown by. I check my mailbox. I have a stack of mail piled high. I take the elevator to the third floor, insert my key in, and twist the lock and walk inside my sanctuary. The first thing I do is get reacquainted with my place. The memories seem vague but the atmosphere is calm and bright. I feel a sense of peace surrounding me. And this feels good.

I walk into the kitchen and reach for my red Kitchen-Aid pot to simmer some hot water to make myself a cup of chamomile herbal tea. I skim through the pile of mail, mostly bills and junk mail. I rip up the junk mail and then toss it in the trash. While the water is boiling I go and turn on old Sis, yeah, she's getting up there in age too. I let her warm-up, and then I check my emails. I have at least 2710 emails in my box. I scroll down each page until I come across one that grasps my attention.

pigeonsimone14@gmail.com　　**A GIRL NAMED PIGEON**

I don't open the email right away. Instead I pull open the left side drawer to my desk and search for Mr. Byren Clausen's business card. I find it hidden underneath some papers. I pickup my cell phone, call, and ask to speak with him.

"Mr. Clausen, speaking." he says in a chipper tone.

Just hearing his voice brings back old memories. I scratch my throat. "Hi. It's Avery."

"Are you okay?" he asks.

It's funny how he still knows me, I think to myself.

"No. I'm not. Mr. Clausen, I need your help."

"What seems to be the problem?" he asks in a concerned tone.

I begin by telling him the long version of my dilemma, which is this bogus marriage to Stacy hoping he can wipe the slate clean resuming back my maiden name…Love.

After we hang up, I find myself pondering in thought as I stare at one particular email address. My curiosity gets the better of me so I click on the email address to see what the email says,

Dear Ms. Love,

So many things have happened in my young life—things that I can't change. Things that I wished I could. I've made some mistakes that I can't take back. I don't have many friends. Actually, all of my friends have dissed me. Who would want to hear what I have to say without judging me, I wonder? It must've been an angel up from heaven answering my prayers, because as I was on the Internet looking up: HIV, I came across www.AveryLovehiv.org, so I decided to hit you up and tell you my story.

I hope I didn't catch you at a bad time. Oh, by the way, my name is Pigeon.

Stay blessed.

A GIRL NAMED PIGEON
by

PIGEON SIMONE

Picture a mother giving birth to her first-born. She has no choice, but to spread her legs to bring her new bundle of joy into the world. Bear with me while I reminisce about my post-traumatic lessons of life. I must relive the past chapters that nearly destroyed my life. Already I am emotional.

I have a vivid picture in my mind of my momma spreading her legs. My momma's misfits of passion nearly destroyed me as a child. Feelings of neglect overwhelmed me and I kept my friends at a distance for fear of embarrassment. Their mommas were respectable women, cordial and caring. My momma lacked etiquette, wearing sponge rollers and a scarf tied around her head for most of the day. Her slippers would be dingy with holes at the big toe and she would wear a housecoat as a dress. She used to sit on the front porch sipping a beer around three in the afternoon. Momma would choke each time she inhaled a cigarette, using her middle finger to flick her ashes in the juice lid ashtray. I would make up excuses or walk like a snail after school so that my friends would end up leaving me behind. My face often turned rouge and I would duck out of sight when my friends would pass through my neck of the woods to get home. I'd hang my head low as momma ignored the signs. She never paid attention to the expressions upon my face. Momma was selfish. Clueless as can be, momma truly had no cares. My heart shriveled up until I had no more feelings inside. My body became paralyzed with numbness and my stomach was sickened by the thought of her demeanor. Fond memories of my childhood do not exist. I was a sad case. Why couldn't my momma be like the other mommas? Lack of attention distanced me even from her. I became a loner in my own home. Whatever self-esteem I had diminished by my locking-in on the zone of self-pity, I felt neglected and abandoned as momma put herself first. Darkened waters surrounded me and I drowned while momma showered herself with attention. Momma fed her flesh with acquaintances, associates, and men who whispered sweet nothings in her ears. My eyes moisten as my unhealed wounds ooze infectious pus. It still hurts me having flashbacks.

Momma was preoccupied with the many facets of entertaining her male guests for the evening. I used to greet them with politeness, as they'd say; "Hello sweetness," and then I would go to my room. Time was allocated and I would greet the next guest. I would then go back to my room where I was able to hear the many moans and groans of, "Ooh baby, don't stop," as they were pleasuring themselves. I used to reach under my pillow and grab my earplugs to drown out the sounds. Didn't momma care that I was in the room next door? Apparently not, she was merely concerned with getting paid. Yep, momma got paid for her performance and I was punished for being born. Momma had no shame in her game. She was a pro. I used to wonder how momma did it. How did she keep track of every Petey, Paul, and Patrick that entered the front door and exited out the back? Momma never took the time to think that possibly her life-style would have a great impact on me.

I, being eight years old at the time, could not and would not speak my mind. If I had disrespected momma she would have cut my hide in two. But deep inside I wanted to ask, Momma, when you gonna teach me how to get a man? Momma would have surely washed my mouth out with soap, if I dared to ask that question.

As I grew into becoming a teenager I became bitter. I understood more than I did when I was eight. My neighborhood clique would tease me about momma. And I had no choice, but to try and defend her. The unpleasantness brewed and I became angry at the world. My temperament was short. My disposition was unapproachable. And I could care less about life because it simply sucked. I began to lose respect for momma and it tarnished my thoughts of me. We never had a mother-daughter relationship and I felt cheated. My childhood bypassed with a blink of an eye and momma never even noticed. The pain was devastating and many a nights I cried salty stains on my pillowcase. Momma didn't have time for me, but she made time for Stretch, Benny, and Ghost. Loneliness made the dingy white walls in our apartment close in on me. I was suffocating and a part of me wanted to die. My life was shattering and momma never noticed. Bits and pieces of my soul were being nibbled away by despair leaving tiny potholes filled with misery splattering the remainder of my body. I became reckless. Folks called me impulsive. I didn't give a damn. Life was too short to be sobbing, dabbing my eyes with Kleenex tissues every night. I didn't have time or the patience to listen to the clock tick-tock, while my life twirled out of control. I didn't see resolution or change in my momma, so I sought the deeper well of darkness. My low tolerance level ignited flames of rage. And I got agitated about every minuscule thing that was in my range. Constantly I stirred up drama trying to coat the real issues within me. People called me crazy, back then, and I didn't care. I had no remorse for momma or myself.

I was the type of sistah who would beat another sistah down if she crossed my path. Mess with my man and you might as well dig your own six-foot hole and dive in. I liked to take risks. Dare me and I was down for whatever, whenever. I was deprived as a child and it had built up into this "don't give a damn about life mentality." I often looked in the mirror at my reflection and a shadow would stand behind me and it would be momma. Predictably, I inherited momma's inconsequential passion towards men. Monday was Gregory. Tuesday was Kevon. Wednesday was Tremont. Thursday was Lenox. Friday was River. Saturday was Elmont. And Sunday was the Lord's Day. My body needed a rest while I would sit in church praising the Lord and listening to worthless gossip by sanctified Christians. Eventually I felt that my tension would erupt and the flashbacks that framed my life would sooner, more so than later, lead me to strike out at momma. It finally happened.

Momma stood in the kitchen one day with her hands glued on her waist saying, "Chile, when you gonna stop prancing around like a slut. Folks are constantly talkin' 'bout you." Momma's eyes were dead. I responded by saying, "Momma, folks have long been talkin'. Haven't you heard?" I twisted my lips. My anger gained momentum as I continued, "Huh? Oh, how could you with all the commotion up in your room?" I was fuming with anger and I let loose like a raging bull. "Momma stops acting like you concern 'bout me! You never showed any bit of interest in my life. Now all of a sudden you wanna care. Don't you think it's a bit too late? Go tend to your playmates and leave me the hell alone!" I rolled my eyes slowly to put the issue to rest, but she'd gotten me fired up. So I went straight for the jugular by craning my neck in as exaggerated fashion as I could muster up, to look toward the clock on our living room wall. I nailed it by adding sarcastically, "Oh, it's almost that time momma, you best go soak in the bathtub with some Epsom salt to tighten back up." I laughed to hide my pain. I recall Momma saying dejectedly as if trying to convince herself, "Little gurllll, I am the momma in this here house!" Momma cut her eyes at me real sharp. "Let me stop you right there, MOMMA!" The words came out with attitude. "'Cause you see momma, it doesn't matter anymore! In times when I cared, you never had the time! When I was feelin' lonely you wouldn't even come to my rescue! I never got hugs and kisses; no matter how hard I tried! I could not compete with dick! Maybe if I had a twelve-inch sausage strapped between my legs, maybe then I'd have been noticed! I am grown, momma. GROWN!" My voice was raspy with emotion and exasperation.

"Now you listen here. Pigeon, I'll slap you silly if you talk sass to me one mo' time." Momma sucked her teeth and puckered her lips. I got a glimpse of her flushed face before she turned away.

"Do what you must do momma, but do it quick." I stood still with no fear in my heart and faced her with my hands glued to my waist.

Momma eyes grew big at my defiance and she screamed, "YOU LISTEN GOOD, MISSY! I am the boss up in here. I pay the bills, buy the food, and keep a roof over yo' head." Momma's eyes looked like saucers by now and her tone was short. "That is so funny Momma because I always thought; Jasper, Cletus and Greyson supported me!" I was boiling hot and was not backing down. I smirked to cover my anguish. Momma raised her hand up threatening to slap me cross my face, but she stopped when she saw that I did not flinch. I yelled out at the top of my lungs. "MOMMA, I SAID LEAVES ME THE HELL ALONE! I'm sure you haven't forgotten how!" I dragged my feet across the hardwood floor, walked into my lonely bedroom and slammed my door. That was one of the worst days of my life.

A few months later Momma died, unexpectedly. I cried with a guilt-laden heart. I was a bastard left all alone—all the other bastards who claimed to be my "DADDIES" weren't a DNA match for me. In my mind I always thought of my momma as being a whore. It seemed disrespectful, but if the shoe fit so be it. My momma couldn't even recall whom she'd slept with last. A clear picture had been etched in my mind at the age of eight, when I was forced to sit around helplessly as momma tortured and abused her body repeatedly with different men. Mornin', noon, and night the cycle continued and she tried to act as if that shit was appropriate. Momma was a spreader and her legs opened to pay for her rent, food, the electric and gas bill, and to put money in her broke ass pockets. She mentored me unconsciously by providing material for me to rehearse every dialogue of hers to perfection. I'd manipulate men with such a great performance I certainly could've earned an Academy award nomination, but barring that, I'd reap any tangible rewards that I could. I was so damned good with the many groans and grunts of fake pleasuring. Well, I'd always reason, whose fault was it anyway that I was a creative, aggressively bitter, young, scornful bitch? My MOMMA's!

Momma cut herself thin back then, losing count of the men who ventured between her buttermilk biscuit. With the warmth of their creamy butter they sopped her up. I suffered and yearned for my unknown daddy. My substitution became any man who was willing to fill the void of emptiness, which more often than not meant my bed for the night. How sad. Yeah, I became the spitting image of my momma with a few perks of my own. My life had been a tornado spinning out of control and I couldn't find my way out. Unfortunately, a way out was found for me. My momma might have been a low price whore, but she was a "smart whore". She obviously used protection with all of her encounters. I, on the other hand, was flying high, loose, and free with Willie, so to speak. Momma died from throat cancer because she had been a life-long smoker. Here I am, seven years after Momma died, and I'm dying because I never cared if I lived or not. I'm infected with the virus. Remorse consumes me now although life didn't matter back then. I didn't feel alive or appreciate the preciousness that came with living. It was common practice for me to wake up feeling fulfilled just by the presence of a man at my side, butt naked in my bed, rather than to appreciate any part of my life. Now I wake up with regrets and tears streaming down the sides of my face. Wishing that I could change the outcome, obviously it is too late. I should have asked momma how she did it, how she protected herself from this devastation. With the Petey's, Paul's, and Patrick's she had done something right. Why didn't she talk to me? Thinking back, I realized Momma probably tried, but I blew her off and pushed her away because I felt she waited too long to try to be a momma. I knew her as a momma who had more time for her bedmates than her only daughter. Oh, how I'd needed her then! I needed her to teach, encourage, support, and devote some of her life to me! I needed the momma talks, laughs, and jokes! I really needed the hugs and kisses! And mostly, I needed whatever love she had to give. I miss her. It is bad enough that I don't know who my daddy is, but I have wished that I could've at least had a good life before momma's death. I didn't. And it pains me so because I have to walk this path of living with HIV alone.

My reality is prearranging my own funeral and that thought keeps a hardened lump in my throat. Sometimes I think out loud, Lord you might as well take me now. I don't have family to help me in my time of need. Momma was all I had. You know what's funny; even though my momma didn't have a job per say, she managed to leave me some insurance money. Momma was smart! If only momma knew how difficult it is to live without her. Yeah, I miss her something awful.

Often I think about how children have impressionable minds, wanting to be just like their parents. But sometimes it doesn't necessarily mean that they have to be exactly like their parents. You see, my momma never truly worked. Yes, she was considered a homemaker, but she didn't tend to her household chores either. I mostly picked up after her. I learned how to cook when I was nine. Momma never encouraged me to be a strong, independent woman. She never displayed any type of passion for anything, except men. She clung to them like they were an addiction. She was hooked on the wrong things and she suffered both mentally and physically because of it. I even supposed she was lost spiritually. All of that turmoil propelled itself in my direction and I lost hope for life. Lost respect for life and myself too. Here I lie staring up at my bedroom ceiling, which is how I often talk to God. Behind closed doors is my time and place for grievance. This whole experience has awakened me. Many may say it's a little too late. Maybe so, but I see other young women living my life. Just the thought inspires me to write and with it, I begin to heal gradually. I am passionate about something for the very first time. And I am willing to share my thoughts, my experiences with the world. I started writing an outline for a column I call, *"Kreepin' Wit' the Virus."* It originally started off as an essay to me. To remind me of all the people I've hurt. Of all the young boys and men I've possibly infected. Actually, it was supposed to be read as my eulogy. Not to praise me but to send out a message to young people that HIV/AIDS is real. I didn't think I would live to see another day. But here I am fourteen years old.

I've been writing about my upbringing and how it impacted my life. How, by me being promiscuous led to me putting myself in the basement. I mean how much lower I can possibly go. Demise is my lowest. I allowed so much to stomp on my low self-esteem. I allowed boys and grown men to play with my head, toy with my emotions, and fuck me until I bled internally. They were just the guns but I pulled the trigger. I did this to myself because I didn't love myself enough. I was a child living a grownups life. And I'm paying dearly. I have no more reasons to cry. I've cried enough. All that I can do from this day going forward is give back what no one gave to me.

I've mustered enough courage to submit a copy of my first column to the local newspaper to see if they'd be interested in publishing it.

A couple of weeks have passed and I hadn't heard anything. I got discouraged and began to understand why momma never encouraged me to pursue a dream or goal. Two days later I received a response in the mail. I stared at the envelope for hours before I got the nerve to finally open it. It was the most passionate and positive response I could have ever imagined. The editor was touched by my candidness. He wants an ongoing column to inspire the adolescent audience. He felt that I would be able to reach them mentally and possibly on a spiritual level. He said that my words jumped off the page, into his heart, and he became tearful. His words brought tears to my own eyes and I cried like a baby. He'd made me feel powerful, appreciated. And with that single letter I'd felt more motivated than I ever had to want more out of my life. His words of encouragement lifted me up. The editor believes in me. He advised me not to concern myself with being judged. That I should be more concerned with helping those who feel helpless I know that feeling personally. I think I cried more because I had no one to share my good news with. It has taken me twenty-four years to finally find my niche in life. Finally, with dried-up tears streaking my face I look up at the ceiling and then down at the floor, not certain if Momma went to heaven or hell. I speak emotionally to her cleansing my soul. "Momma if you can hear me I wanna say for starters, I'm sorry. Sorry that no one ever took the time to nurture you, which only served as a template of neglect for me. I finally got it, Momma. One has to take the initiative in life. You can't wait for folks to come to you. You have to reach out to them. I'm spreading my arms instead of my legs, Momma. I'm writing instead of fighting. I'm living instead of relinquishing my will to live. Momma, I finally got it! It may have been a little late, but you know how they say it's better late than never. I hope you're proud of me, Momma. 'Cause I sure am, I love you, Momma.

—Pigeon

After reading Pigeon's story I am left speechless. I place my hands up to my eyes and shake my head from side to side. Pigeon caught me off guard with her story. She really, really did. This is the time that I wished I still had Anonymous. She is a perfect example of why it is so important to have someone, anyone, to talk to. Where is Xavier when you need him? Not for me, no, I can't think of myself at a time like this. Well, I can still refer her to Red Alert without him, so I do.

Dear Pigeon,

I can only imagine how difficult it must be. Please accept my condolences in regards to your mother. There was a time when I felt totally alone too. I ended up going back to work and I was fortunate enough to land at job at this 24-hour hotline service called Red Alert. It is a service for people with HIV/AIDS to have someone to talk to. This might be something you may be interested in. Everyone needs someone, if only, to lend an open ear.

Let me know if you are interested and I will provide you with the contact information. I hope all is well.

Ms. Avery Love

Within what seems like ten minutes I receive a response back from Pigeon:

Hello Ms. Love,

My name is Tanner, a good friend of Pigeon's. She told me about you—about how she reached out to you and all. Um, I told her that you would respond back, so she gave me permission to check her emails periodically, but after the second and third day she kinda lost faith in you ever reaching out to her. But I told her; I told her that you would. And look, you did (smiling). Her health wasn't great when she emailed you, but she was determined to tell someone her story so... (Deep breath), unfortunately, Pigeon passed away...

It is too much for me to take, so I sign out of my email and breakdown in tears. *God, why?*

***

I bump into Teka again. Well, not exactly. She is across the street from City Hall standing in front of Chase Bank chitchatting with some dark-skinned guy dressed in a dark-colored business suit with a low tapered haircut. They look to be arguing. I am on my way to the train station heading to The HOUSING WORKS BOOKSTORE CAFÉ on Crosby Street, between Prince and Houston in New York, to donate *Anonymous* and *Sleepin' Wit' the Virus*. As I am walking, I notice the guy is tall in stature like a basketball player and he is all up in her face. Now normally I would never butt into grown folks business especially for some chick that I can't stand, but Teka looks like she might be in grave danger right about now. I gaze at my wristwatch, and then at Teka. Wristwatch. Teka. Shit! I throw both of my arms up mid-air, and head across the street mumbling under my breath, this bitch makes me sick!

"Is everything alright, Teka?" I ask her.

Her glossy eyes spread wide. "'Ey, Avery, I didn't see you coming..."

"You o-?"

"Yeah. Everything is great..."

"O-k, because I thought..."

She cuts me off. "No, no, everything is fine. Oh, where are my manners. Avery. JEFF. JEFF. Avery."

I nod my head at him, while he steps nose-to-nose with Teka with belligerence. "Stay the hell away from me!" he says and then storms in the bank. This is a strange Monday.

I decide to go to City Center mall before A.J. Wright goes out of business. I bump into Teka again. Only she doesn't see me. She's dressed in what looks like sweat pants or pajamas talking to some light-skinned dude dressed business casual with a black peacoat on. He has on a snug baseball cap. Now the weird thing is that he is flapping his gums with spit flying out of his mouth. Teka is nearly in tears trying to get him to calm down.

"Listen! Listen! FREDERICK!" she begs. It is most definitely

135

an embarrassing scene with spectators watching and all. Tuesday is full of unexpected surprises.

I happen to go to Unique Thrift store to see if they have any good romance novels. And who do I bump into again? Teka. Damn! She is standing in the corner near the doors by Main Street entrance dressed in what looks like those same pajamas talking to this tall, Hispanic-looking guy dressed in business attire. He balls his fists. She cowers in the corner space. He catches himself and walks off with a tight lip with rage in his onyx eyes. All I hear Teka saying is, "SHAUN!" with her puffy red eyes and snot running fast down her nose. It is odd for a Wednesday.

I'm bored, so bored that I decide to catch a matinee at the AMC Theater in the Garden State Plaza mall on Rt. 4 in Paramus, New Jersey. As soon as I walk up to the concession stand, whom do I see? Teka. Her mouth is moving a mile a minute at this muscular, yellow-skinned looking dude who looks every bit like a fitness trainer. Her eyes are bulging out of her head, as his face is redder than the color. He balls his fists and punches his open palm with it. She literally jumps out of her skin like she is spooked. He walks off as she yells, "JACKSON! JACKSON! Lemme explain…no, no, it wasn't like that…" It is a crazy Thursday. And Teka has on those same damn funky pajamas.

I figured I'd get a manicure and pedicure at Young Nails on Ellison Street. I should've gone on Wednesday for the special. But I wasn't really in the mood. But today I need a little pampering. As soon as I exit the building I see Teka standing in the parking lot dressed in what looks like those same pajamas talking to some guy sitting in a hunter-green Jaguar. He is cussing her out. And she is trying to get a word in edgewise. He ain't trying to hear it. But she won't take no for an answer. "BLAIR, please, please, let me explain," she pleads. It is an awkward ass Friday.

I have a taste for fish, which I probably should've gotten yesterday. I get dressed and head over to my favorite café, Grill 77 over on Washington Street, downtown, and as soon as I step foot in the place, who do I see. You got it! Teka. She is standing side-by-side this brown-skinned guy with a Mohawk and very big feet dressed urban-style. Her eyes are red like she had been crying. She looks on the verge to tears. I act like I don't see her as they head to the back dining area. I go to the bathroom to wash my hands as they are seated at the second table on the left hand side of the room. Teka seems fidgety. And he looks calm. She's nervous as hell. Oh, shit! I think I spoke too soon because he appeared to be calm, but now he is hostile like he's bipolar or something just kicked in first gear. He slaps her, hard. Whack! All heads turn by the sound of it. I purse my lips like I just bit into a lemon. Ooh, I know that hurt, I say to myself. He probably left his imprint on her face. She bawls, loudly, like someone is literally killing her. Everyone is eyeballing Teka, and whispering too. The room is quiet, except for the CD that is playing R. Kelly's song, "When A Woman Loves" in the background. All we hear is Teka crying and screaming in hysterics, "HAMILTON...I NEVER MEANT TO HUR..." she stops yelling when she realizes that everyone is up in her business. Hammer had long left the building. And Teka sprints out like she just got caught with her panties at her ankles. It is too early for this Saturday drama, I think to myself.

I have had enough of Teka for one week! I decide to go grocery shopping at Pathmark instead. A place I know Teka hasn't been in weeks. I roll my eyes at her bony ass. I know. I know that is a cheap shot but Teka is becoming a thorn in my side. Why she is always where I am is really baffling to me. No. Let's not go there. The world does not evolve around me, no, that's not what I'm saying. I'm just saying that... Oh, forget it!

***

I don't know what it is about me, but I always manage to attract attention wherever I go.

Take today as a perfect example. It has to be about 2:30 p.m., and I haven't eaten lunch and decide to catch the 770 to Grand Lux Café in Paramus, New Jersey, to get a bite to eat.

With sweet potato cheesecake in mouth, I notice a distinguished-looking gentleman at the bar staring at me from across the room. It makes me feel a little uncomfortable, especially since I am stuffing my face. Before I can recover, he gets bold enough to walk over to my table. He greets me by saying, "Pardon me for staring, but you look delightful. My name is Mr. Morehouse, Christopher Morehouse." He extends his hand out for me to shake.

I look up, and then quickly grab the napkin to dab my mouth and wipe my fingers before extending my hand in return. "I'm Avery Love."

"Yes, you are." He says with a sly smile.

"I don't mean to pry, Avery, but are you waiting for someone?"

137

He asks, looking around.

"No. I'm alone." I say, hopefully suggestive enough that he'll take it as an invitation.

"That makes two of us." Mr. Morehouse strokes his salt-n-pepper beard.

"Do you mind if I join you, Avery?" He remains standing waiting for a response.

I like his style because he is smooth and debonair. "Sure, you can join me." I smile, trying to lure him with, what I've been told are, my exotic eyes.

He sits and we chat for an enjoyable hour before Mr. Morehouse asks for my number. I open my Burberry purse and hand him one of my old Anonymous business cards. He offers to pay for my meal. I smile, accept his offer, and add a gracious, "Thank you."

I stand, and Mr. Morehouse escorts me to the restaurant door. Like a true gentleman, he opens it, stands and watches me until I get out of eyes distance. He doesn't know that I'm taking public transportation. Why bother to share.

On my way to the bus stop, I replay the scene in my mind. Christopher is attractive. He looks to be in his mid-forties or older. He wears an expensive business suit, Rolex watch, and the telling band of gold on his left ring finger. I remember looking down at the floor as he escorted me to the door, trying nonchalantly to see the size of his feet. They look to be a size twelve and his shoes were fine, Italian leather. This man has impeccable taste. That is a turn on for me.

I know from the very beginning that he is married, but I am not looking for a meaningful relationship with anyone. Who's to say if we will be compatible? Only time will tell. I want someone to wine and dine me. No strings attached because I don't want to get seriously involved with anyone. Not now. Not with Xavier still in my heart. Mr. Morehouse seems intriguing and a part of me seeks adventure. Anyway, nothing can start if he doesn't call.

About two weeks later I do receive a call from Mr. Morehouse. He wants to meet again at the Grand Lux Café so we meet on Thursday evening. Of course I catch the 770 to my destination. Still, he doesn't need to know that I don't own a car. I don't know if it will matter much, but I feel a little embarrassed to share. I enjoy his company. We talk and he is very attentive when I speak. I like that. He doesn't talk much about himself. He just listens to me ramble on and on. I feel very comfortable with him. He asks if he can see me again and I agree. He goes his way and I go mines.

When I get home, I prepare a warm, scented bath to soothe my tingling body and try to relax. I close my eyes and smile. I've had another lovely evening with Christopher.

After toweling off and allowing my thoughts of Christopher to linger, I change into my favorite silk pajamas and pickup the phone to call no one. I keep forgetting, well, not forgetting, but wishing Johnnie weren't dead. I hang the phone up and have a much-needed cry. I need someone to talk to about this new man in my life. Too bad there is no one available to share.

I hear someone scratching at my door, literally. I get up and walk to the door and open it. And you wouldn't believe who it is. Teka.

"Teka, are you alright?"

"Uncle, Uncle Henry!" she calls him excitedly.

"Teka?" I say again trying to get her to snap out of it.

Teka stares at me with wounded eyes, so I invite her in. She's shivering like a leaf. So I lead her to the couch and get Ma'am's old chiffon fuchsia throw to wrap around her scrawny body.

I look her in her wary eyes and say, "Let me make us some tea, okay."

She nods her head very slowly. And then she starts rambling about someone she calls Uncle Henry, again. I don't interrupt her. I let her have her say.

"I was so eager to give him hugs and kisses because he was my dad's very best friend. Daddy and Uncle were close and he was pretty much considered blood. Uncle used to always play with me no matter what game I chose. It was fun because he had a great sense of humor. He was almost like a big kid in grown up clothes. Together we would play piggyback ride and giddy-up horsy. At times, Uncle would sit me on his lap while using his masculine hands to stroke my innocent skin. He would always tell me that I was beautiful, that when I grew up I would be even more beautiful. I was only seven at that time.

"I was comfortable around him because my dad trusted him. Uncle would take me over his house to play with his daughter, Fatima. He would send her outside so that he and I could play touching games. Uncle would touch me quickly, at first, and then ask me to touch him back. The game would go on for a couple of minutes until he touched me in my private part. He then asked me to touch him back in the same place. I panicked, but Uncle assured me there was nothing to be afraid of as he pulled out his penis and began to beat it real hard right in front of me. I watched as he stroked himself until his sickle popped. I felt something was wrong with him exposing himself in front of me, but he'd pinky sweared me that there was nothing wrong because it was natural to pleasure yourself. He asked me to trust him because he would never purposely harm me.

"At seven years old I was naïve and believed that my daddy would not allow me to be around someone who would harm me, so I believed him.

"Every Saturday I would go to Uncle's house to play with his daughter, Fatima. I never told anyone about the games he and I played because he said it was our little secret. He said my parents would not understand the kind of games we played. I believed him.

"As I developed at the age of eleven, his touchy feely became more forceful and I became distant, timid, and even afraid. It happened on one of the Saturday visits. Uncle told me he wanted to show me something that Fatima had left for me in his upstairs bedroom. Once inside the door, Uncle's temperament changed and he became aggressive. I screamed in panic, but no one heard me. He pushed me back onto the king-sized bed and muffled the screams by covering my mouth with those same masculine hands that now seemed like monsters. In my head I was calling for my daddy.

"Uncle pinned me down with the right side of his body, while his left arm reached in my pants and started rubbing my private real hard. He pulled my pants down to my ankles and then he tugged and rolled, tugged and rolled my panties down, which exposed my vagina. Uncle shadowed my frail body with his and got on his knees and unzipped his pants. He spread my legs apart, stroking my inner thighs with his rough hands. I trembled as tears rolled from the crease of my eyes. His eyes became dark and he stroked himself, while rubbing my clitoris.

"My whole body trembled and shook and I pleaded with him not to do what he was doing, but he wouldn't listen. He said, 'Sugar, I didn't hurt you before. I'll be gentle, okay. Just relax.'"

"Uncle brushed his backhand tenderly against my face and moved strands of my hair out of my right tearing eye.

"I pleaded with him again, 'Uncle please!' This time speaking in a soft tone, but he ignored my plea. I wrinkled my face in disgust, and grinded my teeth against the pain that tore into me. I was otherwise helpless as he pushed and entered me until I felt there was no more space in my used-to-be small pocket.

"Uncle rocked and stroked me repeatedly, lifting my left leg up to get a more pleasurable feel, while he teased my budding nipples. I felt myself getting sick to my stomach and in my head I asked God to help me. God make him stop! But Uncle continued to manhandle me and I cringed at his smell, touch, and heavy breathing. I felt my insides ripping. My private, delicate skin was stinging as he stretched it by the many unwanted entrances of his large penis. I knew I was going to vomit. I asked myself again, why is this happening to me? God, please help me?

"There was a noise by the door and I heard Fatima call out for her father. At that very moment I began to struggle. Uncle called to her, 'Comin' sweetie. Daddy will be right there.' He pumped me faster.

"Daddy, where's Teka?" Fatima asked curiously.

"Sugar, Teka's here with daddy, we'll be right out, okay?" He smiled.

"I took advantage of that distraction and struggled and moved my body even more, which made the bed squeak louder and louder. Uncle locked my legs down with his huge thighs to stop me. Fatima was now at the door, demanding that he open it so she could come in and play with us. She knocked and turned the doorknob trying to get in.

"Uncle yelled this time, 'Comin' sweetie! Just give daddy a moment, okay?' He spoke in a rushed tone.

"Okay Daddy." Fatima stood by the door humming.

"At that moment, I got enough courage because I felt safe with Fatima humming right outside the door. I started biting Uncle, hard with my teeth. I kicked my legs up in the air and at him, trying to free myself. Then I yelled. I managed to weasel my way from his grip as he heard Fatima sounding alarmed asking him what was going on. She started banging on the door. 'Daddy! Daddy, open the door!'"

"Uncle panicked and loosened his grip. I asked God to give me the strength I needed to run to the bedroom door, twist and turn the lock with my sweaty hands, until I could finally open it. Breathing heavily and looking a mess when the heavy knob clicked and turned, I ran straight passed Fatima and sprinted out their front door and all the way home. Tears were flowing in the breeze I made as I pumped my legs to go faster and faster until I saw my house. My heart was beating fast, full of fear. And once I reached my house I yelled out, 'DADDY, HELP ME! Daddy, Daddy…he, he-.' Not able to fully get my words out, the tremble in my voice echoed and my daddy came a runnin' to my rescue. He took one look at my face, my disheveled clothes, and the sobs from my trembling body told him all he needed to know.

"Daddy's kind eyes squinted and he said in a compassionate voice, 'Teka, head in the house to momma!' With that said he jumped in his car and sped down the street.

"Till this day I don't know what happened at Uncle's house, but Daddy was arrested along with Uncle. My Daddy was away from me for some years and he never told me exactly what happened for him to be put behind bars. I cried because I missed my daddy. He sacrificed years of his life for me and I am forever grateful to him. I wrote him every day while he was in prison and it only made our relationship stronger, but my heart continued to be weak. I had nightmares. My life was in shambles and I yearned for my daddy's arms to shield me from my demons. He was the only man I trusted.

"Since the age of seven I was being molested by my dad's best friend and truly didn't know. It was a very traumatic experience that left me afraid of the world and scared of most men. It affected me in school and my interaction with people was difficult. My dad's sister aunt Gracious put me in counseling to help me understand what was happening to me and to help me deal with the many emotions I was feeling. My moods would change like the four seasons and often I would fall into a pool of deep depression. For a short time I felt emotionally broken and believed it would become permanent. I was put on medication to help me at the age of thirteen, but not before I was hospitalized for a suicide attempt. I wanted to die because my spirit was already dead.

"My dad's best friend weeded my insides with grief. For many years I blamed myself for his transgressions, but counseling taught me that it was not *my* fault. I was the innocent child. I knew nothing about sex. He exposed his filth to me and took advantage of my innocence. I despised him for it because my life would never be the same. I had to grow up faster than my years and life was pressure living day-to-day. I am confused about intimacy, not knowing how to decipher love and pain.

"Pain to me was like being torched by fire and watching my skin burn. Uncle, a man I loved and trusted, had raped me. He'd tricked me into an intimacy that was a lie and a setup from the beginning, as he pleasured himself. I couldn't tell anyone. Who would believe it? I constantly questioned myself, what is love and how does it feel?

"I walked on eggshells carefully, cautiously, not trying to provoke or instigate anymore traumas in my life. I felt unbalanced hoping to mend myself back into a whole woman. Gradually I embraced the world as my outer layers of skin peeled. I worked diligently trying to heal me inside.

"I was twenty-seven years old when I finally entered the world of dating. I met Malcolm and the thought of him touching me was repulsive. When he brushed his face against mine affectionately, it made me cringe. And when Malcolm looked me in my eyes I could not detect if he was sincere or not. Embedded was the thought of him changing behind closed doors and the padlock between my legs was activated. I was fearful and the nervousness cultivated into an utter panic. Malcolm never touched me in a way that was inappropriate. I anticipated that he was waiting for that unguarded opportunity to make his move. I stopped dating. I was afraid.

"Psychologically that horrific experience has scarred me. For years I was shackled, handcuffed, and held in a self-imposed bondage because I didn't know how to cope with my life. Mentally, I see everything like it was yesterday and I can't seem to block it out. I don't trust people or my surroundings. I shield my body literally, by covering up fully as any Muslim female has been taught to respect her temple, although I don't practice that religion. Spiritually, I am strapped in a straitjacket wanting freedom, but not willing or able to free myself. I desperately want to release myself, but fear torments me and I fall back into weariness.

"One mild breeze of an evening I got caught in the rain and the drops made me feel like I was being baptized. My faith opened up to God stronger than ever and I allowed His shower to drench my body with forgiveness. I had to forgive myself for blaming myself. The worst part of my forgiveness was that I had to face my fears head-on. And accept what he had given me. I had to come to grips with what had happened to me and break the prolonged cycle of living in turmoil. I wanted to be set free, but it was so damn difficult. Weeks and weeks went by and I isolated myself from the world until I got so sick and tired of feeling pity for myself. I climbed out of my well of dryness, and I knelt down to God and I said, 'I'm READY. Lord, I'm ready to set myself free. I'm ready to conquer my demons face-to-face. I'm ready to live my life.' Those very words opened doors that I never knew existed within me.

"The first thing I needed to do was figure out how to begin to free myself from the many years of pain and suffering? Since my molester was still behind bars for repeated charges of molestation against children, I decided the best way to free myself, was to write him a letter expressing my pain and suffering. Uncle may not have a care in the world. He may not even open or acknowledge the letter, but at least he will know he affected my past and present life by just seeing my name on the envelope. Just thinking about placing the letter in the mailbox, sending it to East Jersey State Prison in New Jersey, sent chills running down my spine.

"As I closed my eyes I could see the shackles being removed from my ankles and the handcuffs unlocked from my wrists, as well as my soul fleeing from bondage. Uncle committed the crime, but yet I live in solitary confinement."

I'm at a loss for words, while Teka sits there seemingly in a daze. There are so many questions twirling in my head. Why did Teka come to me, is one of them. I cannot stand this chick, yet she keeps her presence known, why? I guess that question will find its way back with an answer in its own time.

"Teka, uh, you can sleep here, if you'd like."

Teka lays her skinny body down on the couch, closes her eyes, and fades away in her mind.

I sit there deep in thought, wondering what God is still trying to tell me.

***

One week later

Teka and I stay on the phone for hours talking about Christopher, our first meeting, and what I called our first official date. I never told Teka his name. I just call him my man. But I do tell her that he is married.

Teka is also a good listener. She is engrossed in the conversation because she gets excited about everything, especially when it comes to romance. However, Teka is skeptical of me seeing a married man because, as she says, that kind of situation can come back on a person.

I did tell her that I wasn't anticipating any real love connection. I just wanted him to be my playmate. Was it selfish to think that Christopher could just be my toy, there for the pure pleasure of entertaining me? Time will tell.

Christopher is the full package, tall, dark, handsome, hardworking, vibrant, and of course very married. Christopher and I make plans to meet for dinner at Grand Lux Café. He arrives a little

144

late. It seems like he has had too many drinks. I can tell by the goofy look on his face. I've been waiting for about fifteen minutes.

I smile as soon as I see his handsome face. I notice his eyes are bloody crimson like he had been crying or something.

Immediately I grow concern. "Are you okay?" I ask him.

He sits down and just looks at me, peculiarly. He leans his body back in his seat and sighs. "I need to tell you something about me. Something I should've told you long before now. Something I haven't even shared with my wife Karla." *Christopher never said her name before*, I think to myself. He only referred to her as his *other half, they, or she*, but never by her name. This is the first time he's ever said her name. This must be serious, I say to myself. I wonder if he's been drinking vodka. Maybe it's the vodka talking.

His hands meet his eyes as he massages them, vigorously.

I remain quiet, and puzzled.

He scratches his throat, at least three times and by the third time he blurts his words out with momentum. "Avery, I'm…"

I take a deep breath afraid for him. I can't say that I don't want to run for the door and sprint down the highway, because I do. *Not another disappointment like Hellman Middleton*, I think to myself. Not another. From there I take a sip of Chardonnay, swallow, look him dead in his eyes, and then say in a soft-spoken tone, "What is it?" Tears quickly roll down his face as he tries to compose himself. I can tell that it is difficult for him. I reach out and put my hand on top of his and I say in the softest tone I can muster up, "It's okay. Whatever it is, it's okay." I pat his hand with my warm fingers, reassuring him that when the time is right he'll share. There are so many questions that I want to ask, but I don't feel the need to pry.

Christopher leans forward and brushes his soft hand against my face. "You're beautiful," he says. "Um, I guess you're wondering what's on my mind, huh?"

I nod my head.

"Well," he pauses. "Ah, I was born a girl. My parents named me Christen. I was what some would think of as your typical little girl. I was a lively child but something, something," he pauses again. "Avery, when I was twelve years old I-I-I…was raped. It was torture for me. And for my parents who realized that I was different from the children in the neighborhood, school, and church. My parents had a difficult time accepting their only child with this defect. That's what they called it because I had changed. I had a hard time in grammar school and even harder time in high school. No one understood me. Everyone ridiculed me, including my dad. I think he took it the hardest because I was no longer his "daddy's little girl." Some of the girls wondered why I would want to trade places with a boy because all the boys in my school were highly attracted to me as a girl. They always wondered if I was gay. I never thought of myself as gay." He shakes his head from side to side. "No. It never crossed my mind, not until I had my first encounter that I realized how much I enjoyed the taste of a woman. The smell. The soft and sensual feel that women possess. It felt right to be with a woman as a man. It just felt right for me. I never wanted to be a woman after he violated my right to be one. Rape was not an invitation for me. I figured if I changed then I would never have to encounter that kind of abuse again—and ironically I never did as a man."

I take a sip of wine, intrigued with his story.

"But men are raped too, Christopher. They just don't talk about it as much," I say to him. "The only time it is exposed is when a man-of-the-cloth has betrayed them. But most of the time men are ashamed to admit that they've been violated. It is no different from a woman. Hurt is hurt, pain is pain, and suffering is suffering. It's an equal opportunity son-of-a-bitch, you know." *Should I confide in him about my status? Maybe I should refer him to Grand and maybe he can get involved with* HIDDEN-VICTIM COUNSELING CENTER. *Possibly it will help him begin to heal. But how do I go about telling him without making him feel awkward?*

Christopher stammers when he speaks. "I-I-know, but I wasn't thinking about that at the time. I was thinking about looking at my reflection as a little girl. It hurt too much to. I couldn't bear to look at myself as *her*. She was too vulnerable, broken and fragile. Avery, I don't know why I chose to divulge this to you. Woman, huh, you make me feel like I can be myself. I feel at ease with you. It's weird to me because I've never felt this safe with anyone, not even my wife, Karla. No, she doesn't know. I had a sex change way before we met. It was always on the tip of my tongue to tell her, but just the thought of her leaving me left me feeling numb inside. I know that I am deceiving her. I know that it is wrong, but how do I tell her after all these years. After all the times we've made love. After all the times I've tasted her. How do I tell her that she is married to a woman, now man?"

As Christopher is expressing himself to me, all I can think about is Johnnie. I know exactly what he's talking about. Maybe this is why he feels so comfortable talking to me. Maybe my energy makes him feel at ease. I don't know why but I find myself drawn even more to him. Possibly because I know if I care to share about my past he'll understand my anguish.

Our dinner dates become more frequent; my feelings quickly and unexpectedly grow more intense. I begin craving his presence, feeling deprived if a few days go by without seeing him. I am starving for his attention. Yes, me starving for his attention. I have become the fiend for Christopher, not the other way around.

Teka called me the other day and she is still in disagreement with me seeing Christopher since he is married. She feels that I should end the relationship before someone gets hurt. This turns into a cat squabble over the phone and I finally say, "You can call me a bitch, slut, home wrecker, it doesn't change anything. He is my man. He strokes my walls, not yours. He kisses my hand, neck, and even my feet. He runs my bath water, surprises me with dinner, and holds me at night. Here it is three months later and you're still bitching. Who do you have, Teka? Get a Life!" I hang up because I don't care to hear her complaints of jealousy anymore.

I didn't mention anything about money. Money doesn't matter to me. I don't want a man to pay my bills, buy me a car, or a fur coat. I can do that for myself. Once I find a job.

Teka calls me back and asks in an accusatory voice, "Do you even think about his wife? Do you, Avery?!" She is pissed. I can always tell when Teka has had enough. She starts taking those short, hard breaths. I should have never told her my deep secret. But I needed someone to talk to.

"No, I don't, Teka!" I finally counter. "I know nothing about his wife because when he is with me, we don't discuss her." I feel my own pulse rising. Teka won't let up, like she's obsessed with the whole infidelity issue. I say to her, "You know what, Teka? You act like he is your damn husband." I put my right hand on my hip.

Teka still is going on and on. She finally says, "How would you feel, Avery, if you were in his wife's shoes?" She exhales deeply as if disgusted.

I take a moment to think about that one. Then I say, "I guess I would feel devastated. But I'm not in her shoes so why should I care? Obviously, they had issues way before I came into the picture." I pace my hardwood floor, agitated at this point.

Teka speaks slowly and softly as if trying to reason with me. "Avery, you mean to tell me, all these men in this world, you can't find someone else? Why must you have a married man? Why can't you just let him go?" Teka is silent, waiting for a response from me.

"Let him go?!" I laugh because I think she is kidding. She hit a nerve. I try to play it off by saying, "Teka you are seriously bugging.

Plus, it's too late." Damn! I hadn't meant to say that.

"Why is it too late?" Teka asks abruptly.

Teka is sharp, I think. I don't reply.

"Why is it too late, Avery?" Teka waits again for a response from me.

I stammer, "Because, because. I have my reasons." I try to change the subject, but Teka isn't trying to hear it. She is persistent and won't let it ride.

Teka asks defiantly. "Because of what, Avery?! And if you don't answer my question over this phone…"

Unnerved, I shout into the telephone, "Okay! I'm carrying…!" I take a deep breath afterward because I know Teka is going to flip. She does.

"Girl, don't tell me that you're carrying his baby! Have you lost your damn mind?!"

I don't even bother to correct her. Let her think what she wants, I say to myself.

I picture Teka with her mouth hanging open. I start talking, trying to explain everything by saying, "You have to understand, Teka; I didn't walk out the door one day and just decide that I'm going to start seeing a "married" man. It takes two remember? This is where he wants to be." I can almost see Teka shaking her head in utter disbelief.

Teka then says something I'd heard many times before, "Maybe he is just using you because he is able to get the milk for free." I can hear the frustration in her voice.

"He loves me." I say with confidence.

Teka bashes the moment by saying, "Yeah, okay. Believe what you want to believe." Her voice is unsympathetic.

I say, "Whatever." I roll my eyes because the conversation has gotten tense. I walk over to my kitchen sink to get a glass of water. I stay quiet for a moment.

Teka sighs. She says she has a headache and hangs up.

I stand at the kitchen sink contemplating whether I have crossed the line. In my mind, I say yes. In my heart, I say no.

Christopher leaves his wife and moves in with me. I haven't talk to Teka for some months after this and I never invited her back to my home, knowing she probably wouldn't come anyway.

Life is good, anyway, even though we have to wait for Christopher's divorce to become final before we can get married. It is difficult for me. I mean tending to a home, my man, and still looking for work on a daily basis. I am busy all the time. Christopher and I become distant. He starts staying out late, missing dinner, and calling last minute to say he is working late. I don't think anything of it. He gives me no reason not to believe him.

Christopher has been avoiding the subject of marriage. I found a tube of Bobbi Brown lipstick in Christopher's car and he is still staying out late, even more so during the week. Christopher isn't spending much time with me. I sure wish I could talk to Teka about it, but of course I can't. This lie has strained our friendship.

One afternoon I go down to the lobby to get the mail. There is an envelope addressed to me that reads, "Fragile. Do not bend." I go back upstairs, sit at the kitchen table with my morning cup of tea, and open the envelope. What I see brings tears to my eyes; inside the envelope is a picture of Christopher kissing another woman. I am in complete shock. Scrawled on the back of the photo is a note that reads: "He's playing you for a fool. In your face, bitch!" It is signed with a hastily drawn, disfigured shape of a heart.

Who is she? And how does she know that I am seeing Christopher? Still stunned, I quickly take inventory. My life has changed immensely and I can't just walk out the front door and forget about everything I have, we have. I love him. A part of me wants to walk away, and run into the arms of Xavier, I do. I really, really do. But then the other part of me wants to stay. Why should I make it easy for him? Huh, he's the one cheating.

Now I'm feeling angry, bitter, and bitchy. I want revenge in the worst way. But now that I think about it, I can't even remember the last time we had sex. I mean I have to because I haven't had the guts to tell Christopher that I'm HIV-positive. Why? Fear. I fear that he will go ballistic and leave me. Maybe I've grown cold over the years with this shit inside of me. When was the last time I was attentive to his needs? How long have things been this way? I can't answer any of the questions I raised.

Damn! I'll do whatever it takes to keep him. All he has to do is just say the word. I remember how I complained that time when he wanted it from behind, but if that's what it takes, from behind, on top, to the side, hanging from a chandelier, or pipe-sucking, I will be at his mercy. Christopher is my man!

I wonder if Christopher has stopped loving me. The thought hurts. I take a deep breath to calm my fluttering heart, which is beating in distress. I also realize how much I need and want him.

When Christopher comes home, I'm going to fight to get him back. I don't seem to entice or intrigue him anymore. Even when I walk out of the bathroom naked, he has no reaction. No type of arousal. I know it seems over, but I won't let him go. I can't! I start crying all over again. I dry my eyes quickly and developed a plan. I have the scene set in my head. I go in our bedroom and pullout my sexiest, skimpiest lingerie. I pull out my stool from the walk-in closet and stand on it reaching for my box of erotic toys, body lotions, and Christopher's editable underwear. I place them all on the bed.

I start feeling hopeful. I'll make us a romantic dinner by candlelight. Then I'll sprinkle rose petals from the front door up the stairway, leading into the bedroom. I'll take a long, hot, scented bath, and hope that Christopher will be aroused. As he opens the bedroom door I'll be in position on my knees, doggy- style, waiting for him to take me as he pleases. If he wants a freak, I can be that freak, and more.

I hear Avona's voice distracting my thoughts.

Oh, so Christopher gets to have his cake and eat it too, huh, Avery?

SHUT UP, Avona!

Ring, ring, ringgggggggggggggggggg…
"Hello?"
It is an unexpected call from my now distant friend Teka, asking to come by. I am surprised. In about a half hour, Teka arrives. I invite her in, but tell her I don't have much time to talk. Teka seems a little nervous. She says that she didn't mean to intrude, but she needed to ask some questions about my man. Teka has never met him. I figured her visit was because she had come to her senses and realized that this is my life. And if we are truly friends I have to learn from my own mistakes. That's what I thought her visit was about, but here she is drilling me with peculiar questions.

"What complexion is he? How tall is he? What kind of car does he drive? What's his occupation and where does he work?"

"Damn Teka!" I look at her with obvious hostility. "What is it with you and all the questions about my man?" My forehead speaks for me because I am immediately annoyed.

Teka seems apologetic, but continues, "One more question and I will leave it be."

"WHAT now!" I demand sarcastically and glance at my wristwatch.

"What is his last name?" Teka turns away from me and faces my living room window.

"His last name is Morehouse." I calmly say in a confident tone.

150

"Morehouse. Would his first name possibly be Christopher?" Teka turns around, and then walks toward me, and she get all up in my face.

"Yeah, but you said one more question, that's two, in case you've forgotten how to count. Now, what's your problem? Obviously there is something you want to know, Teka, so stop beating around the bush. I have to be getting ready in a few minutes so say what you've come to say." I stand still looking Teka dead in her face, waiting for a response.

Instead, she remains silent, and heads for the door.

"Wait! What did you come here for?" I ask her.

She stops in her tracks, turns to face me, and says, "I'm not who you think I am."

"What are you talking about? You're Teka." I say, slightly bewildered and looking at her with perplexed eyes.

"No." she shakes her head from side to side. "No, I'm not."

"I don't understand." I tell her.

"I didn't think you would. You never particularly cared for her anyway. She told me. She told me a lot about you. She took the time to notice, unlike you."

"What's that supposed to mean?" I ask her a bit annoyed with her slick comment.

She sighs, and cuts her eyes at me.

"What are you saying?" I ask her, moving closer to her.

"What I'm saying is…" she huffs, "I'm not her…Teka."

The closer I get to her, the more I can't tell the difference. "Then if you're not Teka, who the hell are you, then?"

"The likes of her… And everything that looks like her…"

I finish her sentence as if to read her mind. "The twin of her..."

She nods her head with tears rushing down her narrow face.

"Avery, my-my name is Mika. Teka and I were split-up at birth because of the custody battle between our parents. She lived in Paterson and I lived in Washington, D.C. Teka never knew of me, of course, but my dad often spoke highly of her. After our mother died, we met for the first time at the wake and funeral. It was a shock to us both. I mean seeing an image of you standing on the opposite side of the casket is pretty damn scary. It was like looking in a mirror. The only thing that was different was our clothes and hairstyles. Other than that, we were the same person, but not the same. Just two years ago we reunited. Teka confided in me. So I moved back here to help take care of her."

I throw my arms up mid-air, bewildered. "Where is Teka?" I cut

151

my eyes sharp at her, getting annoyed. "Wait a minute… so the story you shared with me was about you, not Teka, then?"

Mika wipes her tears away with the back of her left hand. She lowers her head in shame. "Yes. Sh-she's, sh-she's, sh-sh-she's..." Mika can't even finish her sentence because the pain is so surreal. She begins to bawl like a baby and falls in my arms.

I nearly drop her, but manage to hold on to her before she falls and bumps her head on the hardwood floor. "She's where?" I say, hoping she can compose herself enough to answer my doggone question.

"Sh-sh-sh… asked me to sprinkle her ashes in the Passaic River. She didn't want to make a big fuss. She said something about this is where she belonged. Who would want to be in that dirty water? I mean it didn't make sense to me, at first. I didn't get what she meant by that, though, but as a poet I revised it in my mind of how she looked at herself. Teka looked at herself as dirty, grimy, filthy, but truth be told, Teka was a canvas of natural beauty. And the wrongs that she'd encountered the shame, blame, anything that might've discolored her, degraded her, and ridiculed her; I interpreted those things as her ashes. Her imperfections, flaws, mistakes, which we all have, but often some of us act as if we are superior. No one is superior but God. I now understand where Teka was coming from. It registered with words and emotions, which allowed me to create a poem called "Beauty for Her Ashes." The end result was that she, just as you and I, are only human and vulnerable to love. Teka was a woman of color and complexity. And she was my sister, my identical twin sister." Mika breaks down, but she manages to lift herself up. I'm glad she does, because at this moment I feel useless. This emotional stuff is not my expertise. Mika inhales, exhales, and then sniffs in, while her bloodshot red eyes scan the bookshelf over near the tall windows. "I see you love books, too." She says in a raspy tone. She then walks closer to my book collection. She reads aloud, "*Anonymous, Sleepin' Wit' the Virus*…by Karla Denise Baker. Wait a minute! I read these books…are you…?" Mika's voice rises as if surprised. She extends out her right arm and reaches for one of the books, mouth still wide open. "Avery, you know her…personally? Is this *you* on the book cover? How'd you pull that off?" I nod my head yes. "She asked me to do it for her." I tell her. Mika purses her lips like a fish. "Girrrlllllllllllll!" Mika has no clue that that's my pseudonym name. "I am one of her biggest, biggest fans!" Mika says excitedly. "Did you read, *Does God Have Toys in Heaven* and *I Cried B'tween My Legs: Lust, Love,* and *Life Lessons*, and *Buried*

Within My Rib Cage. She also wrote two other books, um…what were they called," she snaps her fingers, "oh, *Spittin' 'Em Out Like Babies* and *Barracuda Bytch.* I don't know why people don't really know her work. I guess her time will come, you know. Everyone has a season," she says, and then nods her head up and down. Mika eyes continue to travel along the five shelves like a kid in a candy store. "Are these writers from Paterson?" she asks, eyes still wide-eyed and mouth dangling open.

I nod my head yes. "Pretty much. Craig T. Robinson, Jr., *He Was Dying Inside Of Me* was originally an essay that he made into a short story book divulging the anguish that he felt after his younger brother named Anthony died. Lucille "Sissie" Ward, *It's All In My Head- A Schizophrenics Life- A True Patersonians story,* is pretty self-explanatory. I think they are all still trying to get their one break in the literary world. I give them credit, though; because for them being novice writers it shows that they have courage to do something others would say is out of their reach. Some haven't even gone to college. Some haven't even taken a workshop, creative writing class, nothing. Some write about their personal experiences or others that they might know. It is a way for them to heal or inspire others, you know. Some just write from their heads, not from their heart. Some are very passionate about their works. Some are very sensitive about it, too. These are writers that should be acknowledged, especially being from Paterson, but most don't have the means to get their works out like that. Some are pretty local. I guess they all have the same thing in mind; one day they'll make it. To see their works in major bookstores would, I think, be the ultimate high for them. I know it would be for me." I change the subject back to our immediate conversation…Teka. "Wh-wh-when-when did she ask you to do this? I swear I just saw her the other day, in several places 'round town. When did she ask you?"

Mika's eyelashes flutter, then she starts stuttering in a nervous voice, "Uh, she, she, she wrote out her wishes when the time came."

"Time. Time, what are you talking about? Time for what?"

"Why don't you sit down," she says.

"I prefer to stand, if you don't mind."

Mika balances herself and I take a step back.

Mika lowers her head, with her long hair shading her face. "Her untimely death—it took her quickly—she only hurt for a little while."

I gasp.

Mika continues, "H-H-H-Her death? It was an intimate

153

gathering. Teka's dead. I'm so sorry for not telling you the day you invited me into your home. I was just so tired. With the preparations and everything my body needed a rest. And you were so kind. I didn't know how to tell you without thinking about how you'd look at me, at her. She wanted me to give you this."

Mika hands me an envelope. Gives me a tight squeeze, and walks out the door. I go into the living room to sit down. I stare at the envelope remembering when Mr. Clausen came to my home to give me an envelope that Johnnie had left for me. All these feelings of loss come creeping back. My hands begin to shake, along with the rest of my body. God, what are you trying to tell me? I never open the envelope. I don't want to know what Teka has to say. I don't want to relive the pain so I rise to my feet and toss it in the trash, and let the memory of Teka Miller fade away.

As I am just beginning to think about what I am going to do with my life, Christopher walks in the front door. He takes a hard look at me and goes upstairs. I realize I am alone in this relationship. I am on my own. I go into our bedroom where Christopher is sitting on the edge of the bed with his hands covering his face. I walk in front of him so that he can get a good look at me from head-to-toe, and I simply say, "I love you! And I am not about to throw away our relationship, no matter what!"

I stand in front of Christopher and just stare at him. Christopher looks at me and says, "You are a fool. I know your little red secret, Avery. When were you going to tell me, huh? Woman, when were you going to tell me that you got that shit? How you gonna play me like that, huh? After, I confided in you! I trusted you!" I am left speechless. I feel like someone has just punched me in the gut to face my reality. Christopher remains seated on the edge of the bed and turns away as if repulsed by me. His words cut through me like a cleaver and I am wounded inside. In disbelief, I walk into the bathroom and look myself in the mirror, wondering how he found out.

I exit the bathroom and head downstairs to the living room; grab the novel, *Sleepin' Wit' the Virus* to distract my thoughts. I sit on the couch, open the book to page 52:

"I wished I had spoken up sooner before my life became a billboard: www.AveryLovehiv.org," big tears leak upon the page as I fantasize about being in a loving relationship, again. God, how I miss Xavier, I mumble under my breath. I miss him so very much.

A few minutes later, Christopher comes downstairs. He doesn't look at me as he places my keys on the coffee table, walks out the door with luggage in hand; creeping back into the night, probably back to his wife. My heart plummets to the pit of my stomach as I weep grief-stricken.

Within five minutes, the buzzer bellows like an annoying wail. I stand to my feet and drag my listless body over to the intercom to answer it.

TALK: "Christopher?" I say in a crackling voice.

Silence.

Buzz. Buzzzzzzz.

TALK: "Christopher, say something…"

Silence.

Buzz. Buzzzzzzzzzzz.

TALK: "Christopher, I'm sorry for not telling you…"

"Avery, this is not Christopher, it's me, Xavier."

Silence.

TALK: "How do you know where I live?"

"That's not important."

I hear muffling voices so I pin my ear to the intercom. "What are you doing here, JaVonna?" I hear Xavier say.

JaVonna? Is this the same JaVonna that used to date Danell? I don't know what comes over me but I grab my keys and head downstairs to see what the heck is going on. As soon as I get to the lobby I see Xavier with his back facing the door and JaVonna's mouth moving a mile a minute. My adrenaline is pumping. This urgency to do something sweeps across me so swiftly that I don't want an explanation, but feel that it is best not to jump to conclusions.

"Ah, what's going on here?" I ask cutting my eyes from Xavier to JaVonna.

"Avery, let me explain." Xavier says in a desperate plea.

"No. Allow me." JaVonna sneers. "FYI…I *fucked* your man, *bitch*! I'm sure you don't know this, but Xavier can eat my pussy anytime."

I ball my right fist quickly and swing, hitting nothing but air. JaVonna ducks quickly and hits me in my left eye. I feel it instantly swell. Xavier tries to intervene but we are two wild women fighting for our man. JaVonna grabs me by the back of my neck. I can't allow Xavier to see me get my ass kicked so I swing my arms hoping to hit JaVonna in her face, anywhere. I am swinging my arms like a wild woman and kicking my feet. I manage to kick her with the heel of my shoe and I see blood on her leg. I yank JaVonna's hair hard, hard enough to pull a patch of hair from its roots. She lets out a scream that would have wakened the dead. Her face is red with matching eyes. I manage to trip JaVonna with my foot and we fall to the floor with me falling on top of her. I punch her in her face because I am pissed that she came to my house. All of my anger comes out on this bitch and I let it be known that I am nobody's punching bag. We tussle on the floor. JaVonna somehow is now on top of me and slaps me so hard that I know her handprint is on my face. It stings like bees are stinging me, and tears stream from my eyes. The look on Xavier's face gives me the extra strength to pop the shit out of JaVonna's eye...*Pop!* She screeches an *Ouch!* And I continue to swing my arms hitting her any place I can. JaVonna gives me a dirty look and spits in my face. Oh no, she didn't! I say to myself. I grow hot and slap that bitch so hard that I make the ends of her hair fly mid-air.

We tussle and roll about the floor, and then I manage to be on top of her again. Xavier is still standing to the side. I jump up to my feet ready for round three. JaVonna stands to her feet too. We both have a look of rage on our faces.

"Come on let's go, Xavier!" JaVonna demands him and then she grabs him by the forearm.

I look at Xavier, perplexed. "What's going on?" I stand, breathing heavily waiting for him to respond.

Xavier seems at a loss for words.

"Talk to me, baby?" I say to him. "Look, I know that things have not been perfect between us, but I feel I deserve an explanation as to what the fuck is going on."

JaVonna stands with her hands on her small waist, tilting the heel of her Prada shoe as she twirls it around the hard concrete. "Yeah, baby, tell her that you got me now."

Still Xavier remains quiet.

I walk in front of him, nose to nose so that he can get a good look at me from head-to-toe, and I simply say, "I love you! And I am not about to throw away our relationship, no matter what!"

JaVonna rolls her eyes at me. "Bitch, I got your man. He can't get enough of my pussy."

I cackle in front of her face but I feel like she's cutting me up inside. "You may have the man, but just remember I have his heart, and that ain't gonna change. We have a history together unlike you."

"We'll see, bitch." JaVonna retorts. "Why would he give up all of this? Look at me."

My eyes scroll her from feet to face. "All of what?" I say to her as I scrunch up my nose. "I don't see anything but a vindictive slut!

You're still bitter because of Danell. That had nothing to do with me. It was you. You fucked up your own relationship but you can't seem to admit it to yourself." I squint my eyes at her. "What you thought you could get to me by fucking him? I have no ties to him. He is his own person. As you already know, Xavier is a good man and he is entitled to make mistakes, just like I've made plenty of mistakes." I cut my eyes over at him. "I'm sure he's learned a lot after weakening to your trifling ass. I know I have." I walk toward the elevator.

As I am about to push the elevator button to head back upstairs, Xavier reaches for my left hand and pulls me close to him. We are lips to lips. JaVonna tries to maneuver her slim body between us but Xavier blocks her out and focuses on me. "That's all I ever wanted to hear from you, Avery. That's all I needed to know." He says to me.

I shake my head from side to side, "How could you ever question what we've shared, Xavier?"

He lowers his head. I lift up his chin and give him a wet passionate kiss. I look him deep into his eyes and say, "When a woman loves she will go to the depths to please her man. Somewhere along the way we've lost each other, but I know that we just found our way back."

Xavier's eyes begin to well up.

I speak in a crackling voice. "I've never stopped loving you." I tell him in a soft-spoken tone. "Often I've dreamed about you. Most of the time my body yearns to be loved by you. I know in my heart, in mind, in my spirit... that you are 'the one' for me."

A small tear rolls down Xavier's face.

Finally, he knows how much beauty he brings into my life. From this day forward, I will always remind him of how much he is appreciated and loved. No, I can't change the things that have happened in my life nor do I want to, because had none of this happen; I would not know what true love is.

JaVonna jumps into the conversation. "Oh, you think that you're going to get rid of me that easily. I don't think so!"

Xavier turns facing her. "It's over, JaVonna. We are just two different kinds of people—from two different sides of the track."

"What's that 'sposed to mean. That-that I ain't good 'nough for you?" JaVonna forehead crumples and her high cheeks turn crimson.

"No, that's not what I meant. I love Avery and I always will."

"We'll see about that in nine months." JaVonna rolls her eyes and mumbles underneath her breath.

Xavier and I cut our eyes over to her.

"What did you just say?" Xavier says with a crumpled forehead.

JaVonna places her hands on her hips. "That's right, muthafucker I'm carrying *your* baby! What you got to say now?" she looks at him with a sly grin on her face.

My eyes liked to pop out of my head. Just the thought of JaVonna carrying Xavier's first-born is like stabbing a dagger in my heart. That trifling bitch!

"Avery, Avery, listens to me. We only slept together once." Xavier confirms. "I felt terrible after. I felt the betrayal to our love that we share. It really hurt me, so I made sure I didn't fall weak to her again."

I remain silent. I am still in shock that he actually had *sex* with *her*. If her intensions were to seek revenge, consider this her victory. She hurt me in the worst way, but it all will backfire in her face.

Within five minutes, this dark-skinned man comes waltzing through the door with a slew of police officers walking behind him.

Xavier has a perplex look on his face. "Detective Crenshaw," he says, "wh-wh-what are you doing here?"

"You two know each other," I ask him.

Xavier nods his head up and down.

Detective Crenshaw ignores Xavier and approaches JaVonna. "JaVonna Banks, you are under arrest for attempted murder of Ms. Avery Love." He reads her the Miranda rights. "You have the right to remain silent. Anything you say or do can and will be held against you in a court of law. You have the right to speak to an attorney. If you cannot afford an attorney, one will be appointed for you. Do you understand these rights as they have been read to you?" He asks her.

JaVonna eyes bulge out of her head and her voice shrieks with disbelief. "What's going on? What are you doing? Take these handcuffs off of me! What, what's going on? Xavier, baby, Xavier, are you going to let them do this to me—to us—and our baby! Xavierrrrrrrrrrrrrr…!"

My heart literally sinks in my chest. Here I have poured my heart and soul out to this man and now this *bitch* is saying that she is carrying his baby.

As I am about to press the button for the elevator, Xavier reaches for my hand again.

"Avery, please hear me out?"

I want to but a small part of me is saying: enough is enough. Why keep trying this "love" shit. Obviously it is not meant to be. Maybe I need to reconsider being alone for the rest of my life. Maybe I need to see things for what they really are. Maybe I just need to face reality and accept the fact that no man will be completely devoted to me. Maybe I need to just stop trying, dreaming, and waiting for something special to happen to me. Maybe I just need to live for Avery and forget about everyone else. Maybe I'd be better off.

Ding!

I step onto the elevator, and press 3, and then exit off on my floor. Within a few seconds Xavier comes running out of the stairwell, breathing heavily. "Avery, please, please, pleases, *Mrs. Combs*, listen to what I have to say?!"

Now why'd he have to go there? I say to myself. Just hearing him call me *Mrs. Combs* really breaks my heart. Again, I want to hear his every word, just as I want to be his *wife*, but how much more hurt can I possibly take. I try to reason with him.

"Look, obviously you and JaVonna shared something special— something that we haven't. Xavier, do you know how that makes me feel? Do you?" I close my eyes at the thought of them two being intimate. It makes me sick inside.

As I open my eyes, Xavier eyes pierce mines. "I never meant to hurt you. I had no idea that JaVonna and you had a past. I never suspected it. You have to believe me. Listen, all I know is that at this very moment, I love you. You woman, you! You are all I think about, all I want—all I need."

"I hear what you're saying, but there is so much to consider now. A baby? Xavier, you are going to be a father, a daddy. I feel like I have no place in your life anymore."

Xavier reaches in and wraps his arms around me by the waist. "Avery, please, we can work this out. It is not definite that I'm the father. We can work this out together and get a DNA test done. Whatever I have to do to keep you in my life, I'll do. Give us a chance, please?"

I can hear the desperation in his voice. Quickly, I feel myself slipping back to him. Instantly I become teary-eyed. Xavier wipes the tears from my eyes with the back of his left hand before they have a chance to fall down my weary face.

"Baby, I'm sorry. I'm sorry I hurt you. I never meant to hurt you, Avery. I was confused. I got caught up in your past life. I shouldn't have read…*A*—. I should've never invaded your…I'm truly sorry."

"What are you talkin' about, Xavier? What did you do? I'm not following you, honey. What did you do? You shouldn't have read what?" I ask him with a puzzling look upon my face.

Instead of taking the initiative to explain, Xavier simply

massages my back in gentle strokes. I lay my head on his broad shoulder and let the tears fall where they may.

Once I compose myself, I invite Xavier into my apartment for us to talk. "Would you like anything to drink?" I ask him. "A glass of wine would be nice." He says. "I think I have a bottle chilling in the fridge." I tell him, "Have a seat. Make yourself comfortable." While I am getting some snacks together and the wine, my cell phone rings.

"Could you answer that, Xavier?"

"Sure."

He stands to his feet and walks over to the wicker end table and picks up my cell phone.

"Hello?"

"Who the hell are you, answering Avery's phone?" This disgruntle male voice asks.

"Who is this?" Xavier says with a crumpled forehead. He cuts his eyes from side to side looking around at the empty space.

"This is Avery's fuckin' husband! That's who the fuck this is!" the male voice says.

"HUSBAND?!" Xavier voice shrieks.

I flinch, as the flute wine glasses slip out of my hands and smash into fragment pieces to the hardwood floor. My breathing becomes erratic and I feel like I want to run and hide.

"Yeah, muthafucka, her HUSBAND! You tell that bitch it ain't over till the fat lady sings." Click.

Xavier takes a deep breath, walks over to me, kisses me on the forehead, and says, "Talk to me. Do you love him?"

I swallow down a big glob of spittle lodged in my throat. "No." I shake my head from side to side. "He drugged me. He took advantage of me. I'm already in the process of getting the marriage annulled." I tell him with tears flooding my eyes.

He nods his head, then reaches in to draw me closer to him. I smell Dove for Men on his neck. "Okay, okay, we'll get through this. I'm not running anymore." He whispers in my right ear.

"Me neither." I whisper back, in the most sincere tone, then passionately kiss him with all the love I have inside of me.

And in this moment I ask myself, what's *love* got to do with it?

I guess *she* has everything to do with it, because if not we wouldn't be here, at this place, at this time, feeling these feelings that we share. Yes, *love* is what brought us back to one another, and hopefully love will keep us as one: mind-to-mind, body-to-body, and soul-to-soul.

In this moment, something nudges me to look by the trashcan

and as I do I notice an envelope on the floor. I pick it up and realize it's the envelope Teka gave her sister Mika to give to me. Reluctant to open it, I do so anyway, while Xavier grabs the broom and dustpan from alongside the refrigerator to sweep up the broken glass. I reach for a stainless steel butter knife and slice open the seam of the envelope, unfold the acid-free paper that has a green and black flash drive scotch taped to it. I pull back the tape and stare at the flash drive wondering what could possibly be on it.

I walk over to Sis, insert the flash drive, and click on: My Computer as two file names pop up: Anonymous Too and TMS. I click on: Anonymous Too, first.

As it opens on the very first line reads:

"It happened to you, it happened to me…
He put a ring on my finger,
and then he raped what was already his…"

As I am about to throw the envelope in the trash I feel something hard in the corner of it. I open it and pull out a thin gold chain with a topaz rose pearl embedded in it. My right hand reaches for my neckline. As I look at it closely I realize I used to have a necklace similar to it. The evening that I was raped was the last time I saw it. I shake my head no; this can't possibly be the same one. I turn the necklace over remembering that I had had my initials inscribed in it. My eyes widen in disbelief.

There in calligraphy script is:

A. L.